# SPIDER-MAN®

## GOBLIN'S REVENGE

MARVEL COMICS

SPIDER-MAN: THE VENOM FACTOR
by Diane Duane
THE ULTIMATE SPIDER-MAN
Stan Lee, Editor
IRON MAN: THE ARMOR TRAP
by Greg Cox
SPIDER-MAN: CARNAGE IN NEW YORK
by David Michelinie & Dean Wesley Smith
THE INCREDIBLE HULK: WHAT SAVAGE BEAST
by Peter David
SPIDER-MAN: THE LIZARD SANCTION
by Diane Duane
THE ULTIMATE SILVER SURFER
Stan Lee, Editor
FANTASTIC FOUR: TO FREE ATLANTIS
by Nancy A. Collins
DAREDEVIL: PREDATOR'S SMILE
by Christopher Golden
X-MEN: MUTANT EMPIRE Book 1: SIEGE
by Christopher Golden
THE ULTIMATE SUPER-VILLAINS
Stan Lee, Editor
SPIDER-MAN & THE INCREDIBLE HULK: RAMPAGE
by Danny Fingeroth & Eric Fein (Doom's Day Book 1)
SPIDER-MAN: GOBLIN'S REVENGE
by Dean Wesley Smith

COMING SOON:
THE ULTIMATE X-MEN
Stan Lee, Editor
SPIDER-MAN: THE OCTOPUS AGENDA
by Diane Duane
X-MEN: MUTANT EMPIRE Book 2: SANCTUARY
by Christopher Golden
IRON MAN: OPERATION A.I.M.
by Greg Cox

# DEAN WESLEY SMITH

ILLUSTRATIONS BY JAMES W. FRY

BYRON PREISS MULTIMEDIA COMPANY, INC.

NEW YORK

BOULEVARD BOOKS, NEW YORK

Special thanks to Ginjer Buchanan, Ken Grobe, Steve Roman, Lara Stein, Stacy Gittelman, and the gang at Marvel Creative Services.

SPIDER-MAN: GOBLIN'S REVENGE

A Boulevard Book
A Byron Preiss Multimedia Company, Inc. Book

PRINTING HISTORY
Boulevard paperback edition / October 1996

The Putnam Berkley World Wide Web site address is
http://www.berkley.com

Check out the Byron Preiss Multimedia Co., Inc. site on the World Wide Web:
http://www.byronpreiss.com

ISBN: 1-57297-172-X

BOULEVARD
Boulevard Books are published by The Berkley Publishing Group,
200 Madison Avenue, New York, New York 10016.
BOULEVARD and the "B" design
are trademarks belonging to Berkley Publishing Corporation.

PRINTED IN THE UNITED STATES OF AMERICA

10  9  8  7  6  5  4  3  2  1

For Kris

## AUTHOR'S NOTE

The events of this novel take place directly after the events portrayed in the novel *Spider-Man: Carnage in New York*.

# PROLOGUE

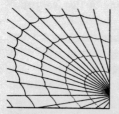

The cold fall wind off Lake Michigan battered at the windows of the plush Chicago penthouse as the last of the day's light faded. The temperature would drop to near freezing by midnight, just a foreshadowing of the harsh winter ahead. The small green trees in wooden planters that had filled the corners of the penthouse's open courtyard had long since been moved to the lobby downstairs. The oak patio furniture had been stored two stories below along with shade umbrellas.

The penthouse had become like a fortress, prepared to withstand the coming attack. The cracks around the windows were taped and the heavy drapes had been shut for days. It was unlikely they would be opened again until spring.

Everything was ready for the winter.

A soft fire flickered in a stone fireplace inside the office area of the penthouse, barely illuminating the oak shelves and leather books that filled the room. An oversized antique desk occupied one side of the office, the high-backed chair behind it turned to one side, empty. A folder, a pen, a phone, and a few scattered papers sat on the desk in front of the chair. On one wall, a bookcase had been slid back revealing a hidden bar. A bottle of seltzer water lay open near a small sink.

With the sound off, the television on the wall opposite the desk cast an eerie white and green illumination that fought with the yellow light from the fire. Deep in an overstuffed armchair a man sat staring at the screen, watching intently what was happening at that very moment in New York's Central Park.

Fifteen minutes before, the phone had rung and a woman's voice had said, ''You'll be interested in what's on the news right now,'' and then she had hung up.

She was right. Spider-Man, in front of a worldwide television audience, was fighting for his life against Carnage, the greatest serial killer of all time. The fight had gone up and down a huge light tower in the center of a crowd-filled meadow like a child's yo-yo, one moment Spider-Man winning, the next Carnage.

The man in the chair had not said a word during the entire battle, seeming to be as indifferent about the outcome as he was to the wind outside the penthouse windows. But he was far from indifferent inside. He hated Spider-Man more than anyone or anything in his life. During the course of the fight he had hoped, dreamed, even prayed that Spider-Man would be killed. That somehow, in some way, Carnage would find a way to defeat Spider-Man, cut the wall-crawler's body in half and throw it to the crowds filling Central Park.

But so far Spider-Man had held his own, so the man in the Chicago penthouse sat quietly and watched.

The door to the study opened slowly and Lyle Robins hesitantly moved a few steps inside. Lyle, a brown-haired, short man with pale, almost sickly looking skin, blinked at the darkness, fighting to adjust his eyes. He had formal-looking papers clutched in one hand, and even though the evening was cold, he was sweating. The papers shook slightly.

After a moment he quietly closed the door behind him and moved over to a position three paces behind the man in the armchair. There he stood, not daring to move.

On the television Spider-Man grabbed a loose power cable and, as Carnage swarmed up over the edge of the platform on the top of the light tower, Spider-Man caught him with the high voltage square in the chest.

The man in the chair could almost imagine Carnage's scream of pain and frustration as Spider-Man held the high-voltage cable against him. Finally Carnage dropped unconscious on the top of the light tower, landing at the feet of Spider-Man.

The camera zoomed up tight on the unconscious form on the tower. It was no longer Carnage, but Cletus Kasady. The camera then moved to focus on Spider-Man as he picked up Kasady and climbed slowly down the tower to the vast cheering crowd.

The man in the chair grunted in disgust and clicked off the television. Then, without turning he said, "Yes, Lyle?"

Lyle gulped and flicked a drop of sweat off his neck. "Sir, the final paperwork on the New York building is finished."

The man in the chair didn't turn or respond, so Lyle went quickly on. "The purchase was done through seven corporations and three holding companies. The ownership was broken down so far, into so many transactions, that it would be impossible for anyone to trace the true ownership."

"You are certain?"

Lyle again swallowed hard. "Absolutely. You are the only one who knows the true owner."

The man in the chair swung around until he was facing Lyle. In his hand he held a revolver with a long-nosed silencer attached. The round barrel of the gun held steady on Lyle's chest for only a slight moment.

"Sir! I don't . . ."

The impact of the first shot kicked Lyle over backward. Without rising, the man in the chair pumped two more bullets into Lyle's body before it stopped tumbling.

The last breath escaped from Lyle and the small man's body seemed to grow even smaller on the carpet.

"Now I truly am the only one who knows."

The man rose from the chair and retrieved the papers from near Lyle's body, glanced at them, and then placed them on the desk. He would have to get another lawyer, and the blood on the dark carpet would have to be cleaned out tomorrow, but that was a small price to pay for leaving no lead for anyone to trace him to that building.

Slowly he moved to the chair, turned his back on the body, and clicked on the television.

An announcer was going over the events that had led up to the fight between Carnage and Spider-Man in Central Park. A picture of a nebbish-looking man suddenly filled the screen as the announcer went on about Dr. Eric Catrall and how his desire to protect a special and very dangerous serum had led to Carnage's escape. The serum was special because even a small drop on human skin would drive the person into a killing rage. There was enough serum in that vial to affect everyone in the city of New York.

The announcer went on describing the details of the day. It seemed that Dr. Catrall had been trying to destroy the serum by mixing it with an experiment to kill the Carnage symbiote without killing its host, Cletus Kasady. But Dr. Catrall's actions had helped Carnage escape. He took the serum with him and it was only with the brave actions of Spider-Man that the city was saved.

The newscaster went on to report that Dr. Catrall was killed earlier trying to escape from a New York jail.

Slowly, the man in the chair started laughing, softly at first, and then louder and louder until even the sound of the wind against the windows were drowned out.

On the television screen the announcer said there was no word as to what happened to the deadly serum. Then the camera flashed back to a live shot of Central Park as Spider-Man swung off toward the tall buildings of New York. It was clear to anyone watching that the web-slinger was favoring a shoulder.

"Thank you, Spider-Man," the man in the Chicago penthouse said between laughs. "Thanks for giving me the last piece of my plan to destroy you."

And then the man laughed again, the sound blending with the harsh Chicago wind.

\* \* \*

The next morning, as the rising sun started pouring in through the bedroom window of his New York apartment, Peter Parker clambered out of his warm bed.

Mary Jane mumbled about his insanity when he got out and then swore at him for letting in so much cold air. It was cold, Peter had to agree with that. And he hated cold. He quickly grabbed a robe and headed for the kitchen. He supposed he was crazy, but there was something he had to do before he could really rest.

After a glass of orange juice, he made a quick phone call, then donned his Spider-Man costume. He tucked Catrall's vial full of deadly serum tightly into his pouch.

Then, favoring a still very sore shoulder from the fight with Carnage, he swung out the window heading downtown.

He had a task to complete.

The vial, a time bomb ticking away at humanity, rode against his stomach. A vial full of enough fluid to send most of New York's people into violent insanity. A killing insanity that would fill the streets of the city with blood. He had taken it away from Carnage, who had wanted to do just that. Now Spidey wouldn't feel safe unless the vial was destroyed, or at least out of his hands. He owed Dr. Catrall the favor of finding it a safe home.

\* \* \*

Ten minutes later Spidey approached the gleaming skyscraper of Four Freedom's Plaza. Like all of New York's most famous skyscrapers, Freedom's Plaza had a distinct look, in this case the stylized ''4'' etched into each corner of the building's upper-floor walls.

Those numbers, as well as the building's address, were symbols of the building's owners and most famous occupants: the Fantastic Four.

A single figure stood in the center of the building's roof, a trench coat covering his dark blue uniform, with white trim and a ''4'' similar to the ones on the building emblazoned on the chest: Reed Richards, aka Mr. Fantastic, the FF's leader and one of the most renowned scientists the world had ever known.

As Spidey landed on the roof, he remembered the first time he came to this site, back when it was the Baxter Building. He'd only been Spider-Man a short while, and tried to join the Fantastic Four in the hopes of making extra cash. That hadn't panned out, but he had worked with the quartet dozens of times over the years and they had proven to be among the finest allies he'd ever had in the super hero game.

He walked toward Reed, one hand holding the vial in his pack like a mother would cradle a new child. He could feel the tension in his sore shoulders and arms. It would feel very good to be rid of this thing.

Reed stuck out his hand, and Spider-Man shook it with his free hand. "Nice job last night," Reed said with a warm smile.

"Thanks. I think I got lucky."

Reed's face turned more serious. "Are you all right? From the tape and news broadcasts I saw, it looked like you took a beating."

Spidey moved his shoulder up and down a little, feeling the pain. "Actually I ache in more places than I knew were possible to ache, but I'll recover."

"Good. I wish we would have been able to get back to help you out. But I'm glad you didn't need it."

"It would have been nice to have your help, but what's important is that this is safe." Spidey withdrew the vial and gently handed it to Reed.

Reed took it and held it up in the faint morning light. "So this is what the fuss was all about."

Spidey laughed. "Besides Carnage getting loose, I suppose so. They say that just touching that stuff can drive a human totally over the edge and into a killing machine. Tell you what, let's not test it."

"Carnage was going to give this to thousands of people?"

"Yeah, the guy is a real sicko."

Reed nodded and pulled a container out of the trench coat's pocket. He pressed a button, and the container opened with a hiss. Reed carefully placed the vial inside and closed the case.

As he did so Spidey could feel himself relaxing.

"I'll make sure this gets into the vault downstairs," Reed said.

"I'd feel happier if you could find a way to destroy it."

Reed nodded. "So would I. We'll see what we come up with."

"Thanks for taking it," Spidey said. He really meant that more than he could say.

"We'll keep it safe."

Spider-Man nodded. With a wave of thanks to Reed, he moved toward the edge of the roof. He paused, inhaling the cool morning air through his mask and reveling in the promise of a beautiful fall day. Sometimes life was good. Today was one of those days.

"Would you like a ride somewhere, son?" Reed called after him, apparently mistaking his hesitation for indecision.

Spidey turned and smiled. "No, but thanks. I know a shortcut home right over the top of that building." He pointed at a nearby high rise. "I'm going back to bed."

Reed laughed. "I'd say you deserve it."

Spidey nodded, and then with a quick wave at Reed, he hit the building across the street with a web and swung out over the street. He did deserve it. And if he had his way, he was going to sleep through most of the day, and Mary Jane was going to join him.

# GOBLIN'S REVENGE

* * *

Reed Richards watched as Spider-Man swung off the edge of the Fantastic Four's headquarters and headed across town. The sun had barely come up and the city had yet to awaken. Low fog-like clouds blew over the tallest of the buildings, letting the sun peak through every so often. The air was crisp with the remainder of the night's chill and the moisture of fall. Reed loved mornings like this, even when faced with what Spider-Man had given him.

Over the years Reed had come to admire Spider-Man a great deal, but this morning he was even more impressed by the wall-crawler. The fight Spider-Man had had last night in Central Park with Carnage possibly saved hundreds, maybe thousands of innocent lives. It seemed the young man was always doing something like that.

Reed turned to go back inside. His mind was already racing on ways to destroy the serum while testing it. It would be a shame to have the good work Dr. Catrall had been doing go totally to waste just because the company he worked for, Lifestream Technologies, had gotten greedy. Catrall had been doing outstanding work tracing DNA causes for human violence. The serum had just been an unfortunate offshoot. And he had had to run away with the only sample from Lifestream, just to keep the serum from being used in the wrong way.

Still relaxed and enjoying the crisp morning air, Reed was halfway across the rooftop when a flash of motion caught his eye. He glanced up just in time to see two round orange balls drop and explode with a hiss on either side of him.

"Pumpkin bombs?" Reed said. "What in the—"

He clamped his mouth shut and began exhaling slowly to keep the gas from his lungs as he ran for the door leading off the roof and down into the building.

But he was too late.

The gas from the exploded bombs had surrounded and overwhelmed him, absorbed into his skin almost instantly.

After two more staggering steps he dropped to the damp surface of the rooftop, protecting the case and vial as he went.

* * *

A moment later, above Reed Richards's still body, a nearly silent one-man helicopter dropped from the low clouds and spiraled toward the roof. In less than five seconds it landed on the surface of the building.

A man, his face and body totally hidden by a white gas suit, jumped from the helicopter and moved quickly to Reed's body. Without even checking Reed's condition, the man grabbed the case from Reed's hand and moved back to the helicopter.

Within another ten seconds the white helicopter climbed back into the fog and clouds and disappeared.

* * *

Ten blocks away, Spider-Man hit the corner of a tall building with a web and then carefully, favoring his sore shoulder, swung slowly toward home and back to a warm bed with Mary Jane. His fondest wish was to sleep for days. Maybe weeks.

He and Mary Jane still were short of money, but for the first time in months he felt good. He deserved a rest and now, with Carnage safely back in the Vault and Dr.

Catrall's deadly serum in the Fantastic Four's vault, maybe he would get the chance.

One hour later he got a phone call which changed that feeling, and any chance at rest for a long time to come.

# CHAPTER ①

 Peter struggled to pull on his Spider-Man costume. The nightmare still had him sweating and his heart pounding like it wanted out of his rib cage. Every time he had tried to sleep, or even nap, over the last two weeks the nightmare had come back. It had become a regular part of his life and there didn't seem to be anything he could do about it.

*Red. Blood everywhere, like paint splattered by children. He hung from the side of a building, his hands sticky from the blood, his costume dripping blood. If he shot a web, it would be a string of blood.*

*Below him the streets of New York were covered at least two stories deep in mutilated bodies. The faces, eyes open, stared up at him, asking him why he didn't do more to help them.*

*Why he didn't save them?*

*They all blamed him. Their gazes followed him. Millions of eyes staring at him.*

If he didn't wake up at that point, the nightmare would continue.

*The mutilated bodies flowed into one another, forming a huge mass of red and black. A river of blood flowed between the buildings.*

*A face took shape on the surface of the river of blood. . . .*

And Peter would wake up, sweating. Not once had he made it beyond that point in the nightmare and not once had he recognized the face forming in the blood.

But over and over, the nightmare came back. No matter

how tired, no matter how much he needed sleep, the nightmare stopped him. It was as if he were punishing himself for giving the serum to Reed and then it being stolen.

At least that was Mary Jane's theory.

If he had just kept it, or destroyed it, the serum would not be a threat to the city.

He finished pulling on his costume, all except his mask and gloves, and took a few deep breaths to calm his nerves. From the kitchen he could hear the sounds of Mary Jane cooking herself a late breakfast. He'd been out all night guarding the city and when he'd come to bed he had woken up Mary Jane. The clock on the bed stand told him he'd been asleep for less than an hour, but that was the longest amount of sleep he'd had in the last two days.

He wandered into the bathroom and tossed a handful of cold water on his face. His eyes felt like a constant sandstorm was filling them with grit, and the circles under his eyes had gone from a faint brown to a dark black, almost as if he had two black eyes.

"You're a mess, Peter," he said to his reflection. "The question is what to do about it."

He splashed his face again with another handful of cold water and then took a deep breath. But the vision of the river of blood still filled his mind.

It had been two weeks since someone had stolen Dr. Catrall's deadly serum from Reed Richards. Two long weeks of days and nights guarding the city, searching for any clue, working with the Fantastic Four and anyone else who offered to help. Two weeks of no sleep and the same nightmare. Thousands of dead blaming him. A river of blood in the streets. And the face in the blood. It was as if the nightmare, or his subconscious, as Mary Jane told him, was trying to tell him something. He didn't know what it might be, other than guilt, and he could never stay in the dream long enough to see whose face formed in the blood.

From the honking sounds outside, at least the city was still safe. For the moment.

"What are you doing?" Mary Jane asked from the bathroom door. Her voice was firm and Peter could tell she wasn't happy with him being awake.

He turned toward her. She was leaning against the doorframe. Her long, beautiful red hair cascaded over her shoulders, touching the front of the apron she wore over a white blouse and jeans. Every so often Peter was struck by just how beautiful his wife was and this morning, through all the tiredness, was one of those times.

"You're beautiful when you're upset."

Mary Jane shook her head no. He could tell she wasn't going to let his compliments sidetrack her, no matter how well-meaning they happened to be.

"You promised me you'd rest for at least three hours."

"Nightmare," Peter said as he moved past her back into the living room. Just saying the word brought the picture of the stacked bodies and the blood flowing like a river down Broadway into his mind.

And the face. The face in the blood.

If the serum was in the wrong hands, as was fairly likely, all things considered, that nightmare might well turn out to be very, very real. He kept telling himself that if he kept going, kept moving, kept guarding the city, that wouldn't happen. It was the only thing he could think to do.

He pulled on his gloves, making himself concentrate on the activity to again shove the nightmare to the back of his mind. Sometimes that worked, but not this time.

Mary Jane moved over and put her arms around him. ''You know it's the lack of sleep that's feeding the nightmare.''

''That,'' Peter said, ''and fear.''

Mary Jane nodded and hugged him. ''Yeah, that too,'' she said, softly. ''That too.''

Peter let himself stop for a moment and enjoy Mary Jane's hug. Having her understand really helped. It was almost as if she took the nightmare from him and drained it away.

He let himself enjoy her pressing against him for a moment longer, then turned to face her. ''I gotta go.''

Mary Jane nodded. ''Of course. But you need some food. I've fixed some breakfast.''

''Thanks,'' Peter said. ''You go ahead, but save me some. I'll be back in a few hours at most.''

''I'll make you a sandwich when you get back.'' Then she pulled him close and kissed him. ''Be careful.''

''I always do my best,'' he said. He smiled his tired smile at her, then pulled on his mask and moved to the window. His spider-sense told him it was clear and without looking back he hit the building across the street with a web and was on the way downtown, over the still-dry, blood-free streets.

\* \* \*

Mary Jane watched him go, the worry twisting in her stomach. She'd been afraid for Peter's life numbers of times over the last few years. In fact, every night he was

20

out being Spider-Man she worried. But this time seemed different. He'd always been driven, but never to this length. She could not remember him being this tired and upset since—well, since Gwen Stacy died.

She watched him move over the top of the neighboring building and then turned and moved back to the kitchen and the phone. The morning paper was spread out on the counter, open to the want ads. She'd been looking for a job, any job for the short term. They were almost out of money, and with Peter being so focused on finding the serum and whoever stole it, he wasn't even taking pictures for the *Daily Bugle*. And no acting jobs had opened up for her yet. So maybe she could go back to waiting tables. Peter would hate it, but it would be the least she could do to help him.

She moved to where she had made breakfast for herself and began fixing Peter a sandwich. Maybe someday soon she'd find acting work again and they could afford to go out to a nice restaurant. But for the moment, every penny counted and they couldn't afford much more than sandwiches. That was one drawback to what Peter did. There wasn't any money in the super hero business.

\* \* \*

Worrying about money was the farthest thing from Spider-Man's mind as he approached Four Freedom's Plaza. He was focusing on hitting each web exactly where he aimed, fighting through the exhaustion that threatened to overwhelm him. Also, focusing on the job of going from one building to another kept his mind occupied enough to not think about the face in the blood. Or at least not think about it all the time.

As Spider-Man dropped onto the surface of the Fantastic Four's building, Reed came out the rooftop door and moved toward him.

"Anything?" Reed asked, offering his hand.

Spidey accepted Reed's offered handshake. He took assurance from Reed's firm grasp. There was just something about Reed Richards's tall, thin frame and broad shoulders that inspired confidence in those around him, and at the moment Spidey knew he needed as much confidence as he could get.

"Don't I wish," Spidey said and then watched as Reed frowned. Spider-Man knew that Reed and the rest of the Fantastic Four had gotten as little sleep as he had, searching for the person who stole the serum. And they had had the exact same amount of luck coming up with answers in the last two weeks as Spidey had: zero.

Reed turned and paced, his hands behind his back, his dark blue uniform catching the light as he moved.

Spidey made himself take a deep breath of the cool fall air. It didn't help. His eyelids still felt like they were lined with sandpaper and every time he blinked he could see the face forming in the river of blood.

"Maybe we're going about this wrong," Reed said, stopping his pacing and facing Spidey.

"I don't think we should pull the guards off the city water supplies," Spidey said. He couldn't even believe Reed would think of such a thing.

Reed held up his hand. "I don't either. And that's not what I'm talking about. I think we should go back to the only evidence we have and start from there."

"The pumpkin bombs?" Spidey said. "We've talked about that before. Norman and Harry Osborn, the original

Green Goblins, are both dead. And Jason Macendale is still safely tucked away in his cell,'' he said, referring to the Hobgoblin.

Reed nodded. "But what if someone else found a cache of Norman or Harry's old Goblin supplies?"

The face of Norman Osborn, the first Green Goblin, came back to Spidey as clear as if Norman was standing there. Then the face of Harry, his son. Harry had been Peter's best friend and roommate for years before he followed his father into insanity.

Spidey took another deep breath. Then as always happened when he thought of the Green Goblin, the face of Gwen Stacy filled his mind. Gwen Stacy, Peter's old girlfriend. And as tired as he was he couldn't stop rerunning the scene of her dying after the Goblin pushed her from the Brooklyn Bridge.

Reed turned and took a few steps toward the edge of the building so he could stare out over the city. "I did some investigating through sources at Lifestream Technologies. It wasn't easy, but I discovered that the serum that Dr. Catrall was working on came from a formula initially developed by Mendell Stromm."

"What?" That cleared Spidey's mind of thoughts of Gwen. He moved quickly to Reed's side. Just the mention of the name Mendell Stromm sent shivers running down Spidey's back. Stromm had developed the serum that gave Norman Osborn the powers of the Green Goblin. Extra strength and the ability to hit very, very hard. And it had been that same serum that had finally driven Norman, and later Harry, completely crazy.

So if Catrall's serum was an offshoot of Stromm's, no wonder it was so dangerous.

Reed didn't look around at Spidey, but instead kept staring out over the city. "The only hard evidence we have is that pumpkin bombs were used to steal a serum similar to one used to originally create the Green Goblin. Odd, wouldn't you say?"

"Very odd." Spidey forced his tired mind to work. It did seem like a clear connection, but for what reason and for what use? "So we have a connection. But does that lead us anywhere? Do we have something to tie the serum and the pumpkin bombs to a person or group?"

"Not a thing," Reed said. "I even went back and did more tests on the remains of the pumpkin gas bombs. They are exactly the same as the Green Goblin used." He turned to face Spider-Man. "Exactly."

Spidey nodded, getting what Reed was saying. "So two questions. Where did the person who stole the serum get the Goblin's pumpkin bombs?"

Reed shook his head. "No answer yet."

"And did he or she know that Catrall's serum was similar to Mendell Stromm's?"

Again Reed just shook his head at Spidey's question. "We find the answer to those two questions and we have our thief."

Spidey nodded. "I agree all the way. But we're back to the same old thing: What next?" Spidey laughed, even though there was nothing funny about it. "That seems to be the only question I've asked for the last two weeks."

Reed chuckled. "Indeed." He pointed down at the street below. "However, if I were you I'd make it a priority to stay away from the government boys for the short term."

Spider-Man glanced at the drab, government-looking car parked on the street below. "FBI?"

Reed nodded. "Likely."

"They still think I might have had something to do with the serum getting stolen?"

Reed shrugged and continued to stare at the car. "Life-stream was very annoyed that you didn't return the serum to them when you got it back from Carnage. And they have a great deal of influence in Washington."

"Enough to get the FBI out against me?"

"And us too," Reed said.

Spidey shook his head in disbelief and stared at the car. His spider-sense didn't tingle at all, so for the moment there was no danger. But he sure didn't need the FBI butting into his life, trying to find the thief of the serum. That was just one problem too many.

"They're going to have to learn how to fly if they want to catch me," Spidey said.

Reed patted the web-slinger on the back. "Just be careful. We need you on this one."

"I will," Spider-Man said. Having Reed Richards tell him he was needed gave him a boost of energy. "Tell you what. I'll check out some of Osborn's old buildings just to cover that base."

"Good," Reed said. "I'll keep working on the Life-stream side. And for the moment everyone is staying on their patrols and guard stations. The city is as safe as we can make it."

"I wish that thought would let me get some sleep."

Reed only nodded in reply.

"I'll let you know what I find," Spider-Man said as he hit the neighboring building with a webline and swung off. For the moment he felt as if he had some energy and a real task. Two weeks of fear and waiting had been driving him nuts. At least this gave him something to do.

* * *

Two hours later he crouched on a building ledge overlooking the *Daily Bugle*. The fall wind was cutting at his face through the mask and his hands and feet were already cold. And it still wasn't anywhere near noon.

He had checked ten of the old Osborn properties scattered around the city. Eight of them were occupied by one company or another and all but one of them had been completely remodeled a number of years back. Not much chance that anything had been found in them.

One building was being torn down and Spidey had spent almost an hour going through what was left, looking for any signs that the workers had uncovered a secret room full of Goblin supplies. Nothing.

Osborn's old corporation headquarters building was empty. Spidey had gone in through the roof of the empty main building and worked his way to the street, looking for any sign of activity.

Again nothing at all. The place had been abandoned since right after Harry died, and a thin layer of dust coated almost everything. Only a few street people had gotten in on the main floor through a broken and boarded-up window.

It had felt odd to Spidey to be inside that building again. All the years of Norman and Harry there seemed to fill it with too many ghosts for Spider-Man. Ghosts of Harry and of Gwen.

Only the bones of the past remained. Harry was dead.

Gwen was dead. The Osborn building was dead. It all fit in a sad sort of way.

Reed's discovery of a connection between the pumpkin bombs and Dr. Catrall's serum had been the first real progress they had had in two weeks. But unless they found that next connection, they were right back to where they had started. Nowhere.

Spider-Man let his tired eyes study the crowd going in and out of the *Daily Bugle's* front door. It had been two weeks since he'd even thought of taking a picture. J. Jonah Jameson was going to be angry almost beyond words. Peter had worked himself into a position of top-level photographer at the *Bugle*. So for him to suddenly not be around for two weeks was not going to make anyone happy.

He was debating whether to change and go inside or go home and try to take another nap when a man in the crowd below caught his attention.

Spider-Man blinked a few times to clear the tiredness from his eyes and let the cold air flush them out. Then he looked again.

Walking slowly through the crowd below, moving away from Spider-Man and toward the old Osborn building down the street, was a man wearing a long coat and an older-fashioned brimmed hat. From the side the guy looked like Norman Osborn.

*You're finally flipping out*, Spidey decided. *Osborn has been dead for years.*

But somehow even his own thoughts seemed hollow.

Spidey webbed across to the *Bugle* building and then ran across its roof. He jumped quickly to the next building up the street so that he could get a better look at the guy's face.

He went quickly down the side of the building to a place two stories over the sidewalk. It took a moment to spot the guy again in the heavy crowd, but when Spider-Man did, he gasped. From face all the way down to the clothes it was Norman Osborn. Or a dead ringer for him.

Same type of clothes. Same short haircut.

Same scowl on his face.

Norman Osborn.

Or his ghost.

*Could Norman have had a long-lost brother?* Spidey rubbed his eyes through his mask, trying to clear them. The man who looked like Norman Osborn turned into a hotel entrance, moving without hurry with the crowd.

*Don't lose him!* Spidey dropped toward the ground. At the last instant he hit the hotel sign with a web and swung over the street just above the car tops, and onto the side of the hotel over the door.

The guy who looked like Norman Osborn was already inside.

Spider-Man dropped to the sidewalk, sending ripples and murmurs through the crowd as everyone moved back to give him room.

With a quick push, Spidey was through the revolving door and looking over the large lobby of the hotel. The place was huge, with marble walls and two-story stone pillars. The people entering moved from the door down three steps and into a huge lobby. The guy hadn't had time to even get across it. Yet he was nowhere to be seen.

Slowly the hundreds of people in the lobby stopped what they were doing and turned to stare at Spider-Man.

Spidey waved and then scampered up a large stone pillar inside the lobby so he could get a better view of the room.

The guy was gone.

Completely.

As if it really *had* been Norman Osborn's ghost.

"Sorry to disturb you, folks," Spidey said.

He quickly dropped to the lobby floor and went out the door. Something about this nagged at the back of Spidey's brain. Something had just happened that he knew was important, but he didn't know exactly what. This disappearing act seemed familiar somehow, but he was so tired he couldn't figure out to what or where it fit.

"You need sleep," Spidey said as he went up the side of the hotel.

A moment later he was over the top of the *Bugle* building and headed for home. Nightmare or not, he was going to sleep. When he started imagining that he was seeing Norman Osborn walking the street just because Reed Richards had suggested a connection, he needed rest.

And lots of it.

\* \* \*

The hotel's revolving door let go of a man dressed in a formal three-piece suit. The man stepped to one side and stood on the sidewalk with his back against the building watching as Spider-Man disappeared over the top of the *Daily Bugle*.

Then, slowly, softly, the man started to laugh.

It would have been a very familiar laugh to Spider-Man if he had been close enough to hear it.

# CHAPTER (2)

The small briefing room was overcrowded and hot. Located four stories beneath Lifestream Technologies World Headquarters, no open window could cool the room and the small ventilation system wasn't designed for a quick turnover of air. Normally the gray-painted room was used for storage of office supplies and copy paper. But today all the supplies had been stacked along the wall in the halls to make room for twenty-five folding chairs, a small podium, and a map of the city that covered the wall behind the podium.

Twenty-five men had crowded into the room at ten minutes before ten in the morning and taken their seats facing the podium and the map. All wore similar-looking gray-toned suits, dark ties, and polished black shoes. All were in their mid-twenties, in good physical condition, with close-trimmed hair, and clean-shaven faces.

As the heat grew in the room not one man moved to loosen his tie. They sat, mostly facing forward, waiting.

Some men had been talking softly among themselves, but that stopped instantly as, at exactly ten, a man in an expensive three-piece suit entered and strolled to the small podium. His suit was a rich dark blue and he wore a light blue tie. The suit and tie were the only color in the room.

The silence was complete as the man at the front looked down at the twenty-five seated men.

K. L. Bogal was his name and he was known to every man in the room as a feared and dangerous mercenary. He had been known to kill a man almost without moving and some said his gaze could cut a man into pieces. He had no known vices, unless a ten handicap at golf was a vice, and Bogal would probably have killed anyone who suggested it might be.

Bogal had been hired by Lifestream Technologies to get the serum stolen by the late Eric Catrall back into the Lifestream labs. His instructions were clear. There was no cost too high. He had been given a free hand and an un-limited budget, just the way he liked it.

He did not intend to fail.

His personal history was clouded in rumor. Some said he had worked for the CIA. Others said he'd been with the mob. One rumor even had him as an ex-boxer with a deadly left hook. But no one really knew and Bogal never told. He just did his job, quickly, efficiently, and perfectly. And those who got in his way vanished, usually without a trace or a sound.

"Gentlemen," Bogal said, finally breaking the silence in the stuffy room. His voice was firm, low, and full of authority. A voice no one ever argued with. "You have all been picked by me for your ability to follow orders. I will not be happy if I discover I have made a bad choice."

He let the silence drive his message home through the hot air. Not one man said a word, so he continued.

"Lifestream has given us the task of retrieving a vial of extremely important and dangerous serum stolen by an employee. The employee is now dead. The last person seen with the serum was Spider-Man, so we are going to start with him."

Bogal turned to the wall and the black and white city map as the men stirred at the mention of Spider-Man's name. "We will stake out the roofs of twenty-five of the city's main buildings.'' His finger stabbed the map, noting buildings in the very center of town, before he turned back to face the men. ''We will track Spider-Man until he leads us to the serum.''

Around the room heads nodded in understanding.

''And,'' Bogal said, waiting a moment to let his words be the only thing of focus in the room, ''if Spider-Man will not lead us to the serum, we will capture him. Then he will take us to it, I promise you.''

Ignoring the reaction of the men, Bogal gestured in the direction of the open door. A man came in carrying what looked to be a jet fighter's helmet. It was a shiny black, and very futuristic looking.

Bogal took the helmet and held it up for all to see. ''A recent development in night vision allows us to track and record at any time of the day or night as if it is full daylight.'' Bogal pointed to the lens of the helmet. ''It constantly keeps the amount of light level to the cameras inside.''

''Full communication capabilities,'' he said and pointed to the ear areas of the helmet. ''And full computer tracking of anything moving within a three-hundred-yard radius.'' He pointed to the bulge above the lens. ''Everything this helmet sees is relayed instantly back to the central computer and map room. From there, I will keep track of all sightings, and trace Spider-Man's movements.''

He handed the helmet back to the man. ''You will be dispatched in two-man teams. Every team will have a helmet, and one member will wear it constantly every minute of every day. That way each team will be in contact with every other team and the main computer every second of every hour of every day.''

He paused for a moment, letting his words sink in. ''There will be no place in the center of this city that Spider-Man can go without us knowing about it.''

He leaned forward for effect. ''Understand me. No place.''

Again the heads around the room nodded, this time slightly more enthusiastically.

Bogal gestured at the door and another man in a gray suit and dark tie entered carrying what looked to be a very wide-barreled rifle with a scope. The man handed the rifle to Bogal who held it up for each man to see.

''This is a sonic rifle, another new invention. It will be the only weapon any of you will carry. It fires a stunning beam over three hundred feet through any material. The beam can be adjusted for wide or narrow spray.''

Bogal held the rifle over his head. ''Anyone in the path of this weapon when fired will be hit with a massive case of vertigo, and will pass out. Anyone. Including Spider-Man.'' Bogal waited a moment, then continued. ''There will be a bonus of twice your salary for the team who captures Spider-Man alive. But be warned,'' Bogal pointed the rifle at the men, ''if Spider-Man is hit with this sonic beam and passes out thirty stories in the air, he will fall to his death. I will personally kill the man who kills Spider-Man.'' Bogal made a rifle recoiling motion with the gun and then handed it back to the man who carried it in.

''Understand?''

Not a man in the room even blinked, so Bogal went on. ''Good. Now report to the training center one floor down. I expect everyone to be fully efficient with both these devices by tomorrow morning. Dismissed.''

As the men rose, Bogal held up his hand for attention and everyone froze. ''One more thing. Get a good night's sleep. It may well be your last for some days to come.''

He nodded dismissal and the men again began to move toward the door.

*     *     *

The man from Chicago sat alone, behind the huge oak desk in the only chair in the room. He was now three stories underground, in the basement of a large New York office building, seeming light-years from his plush Chicago penthouse.

One small desk lamp illuminated the large, old office. The books in the shelves hadn't been touched in years and dust covered everything but the chair and the desk with a fine gray layer. The air smelled stale and dry. Up until three weeks ago the room had been sealed and very well hidden. Not even the rats had found their way in here, though a cockroach or two had snuck in.

The man leaned back and held a small vial of serum up to the light. The fluid in the vial caught the light in a slight rainbow pattern. The man studied it for a moment and then placed the vial back into its small case on top the desk.

''Events are in motion, my friend,'' the man said to no one. His voice was swallowed by the dry air and the dust. ''Soon your death will be avenged, as I should have done the first time. That much I promise.''

The man left the case open and leaned back, glancing around the room, admiring his find. He couldn't believe his luck. If not for the computer belonging to Sergei Kravinoff, a.k.a. Kraven the Hunter, this room may have stayed hidden for years. Now, from this room, from this building, he would make sure that Spider-Man paid his debts.

Spider-Man would pay for the death of Kraven. First with his sanity and then with his life.

The buildup to this moment had taken a long time.

The man from Chicago leaned back in the chair and thought over the events. It had been months after Kraven the Hunter died before the man had dared return to the old mansion.

He hadn't known why he was returning. He just knew he had to. It had been lucky that he did. He'd stumbled on a secret room with a computer still running. On the computer buried in the remains of Kraven's destroyed mansion he had found information about Spider-Man and the original Green Goblin. The man from Chicago had discovered many things from that computer. Things he needed to know to kill Spider-Man and avenge Kravinoff's death.

It had taken him days in those ruins, but he had learned that Spider-Man had almost gone insane after the original Green Goblin killed Gwen Stacy. There was no mention of any connection between Gwen Stacy and Spider-Man, but obviously, from Spider-Man's reaction, there must have been.

The man from Chicago discovered that Harry Osborn, Norman Osborn's son, had become the second Green Goblin and had also gone insane.

He learned that the two Green Goblins were among Spider-Man's most deadly foes. He also learned that the serum that transformed the Osborns into such power-houses was developed by Mendell Stromm. Stromm's work was continued by Dr. Eric Catrall at Lifestream Technologies, the same Eric Catrall who was killed after Carnage stole the serum.

And from that same computer in the basement of that destroyed mansion the man learned of this room and the bigger one beyond it. The only two rooms owned by Norman Osborn not found and looted by the Hobgoblin. Two rooms not even known to Harry Osborn. In fact, it was doubtful that even Norman Osborn had remembered these rooms in his last, insane days. He had been driven to the brink of madness from the long-term effects of Stromm's serum, and the records showed that in those last few days before he was killed he went over that brink.

It had taken the man from Chicago a very short time to buy the building. And now he was sitting in the hidden office, almost ready.

Ready to finally watch Spider-Man die.

The phone in the man's jacket pocket beeped softly, cutting into his memories and plans for revenge. He pulled out the cell phone, opened it, and listened for a moment. Then he said, "Go ahead. And do not fail me."

He closed up the phone and laid it beside the vial of serum. He stroked the vial reverently for a moment, as if it were his favorite pet. A pet that could kill millions.

"Soon," the man said to the vial. "Soon you will be put to good use. Soon you will force Spider-Man to face himself and his worst fears. Soon."

The night at Kraven's mansion flooded back into the man's mind like it had happened yesterday. The cold wind, the darkness.

And his own reactions. He had broken at Spider-Man's hands. He had backed away from his convictions to avenge his friend Kraven. Spider-Man had beaten him and then, like he would have done to a small child, let him live.

The flush of the humiliation flooded over him. That wouldn't happen this time. He wouldn't run this time. He would fight Spider-Man to the death if he had to.

The man closed the lid of the case over the vial and shook off the anger that night's memory had brought up. He had to keep his head clear and keep thinking. It would be the only chance he had of defeating Spider-Man.

"It's time for more practice."

His words echoed around the old office as the man stood and moved across the room to a heavy metal door. On the other side was a large, hangar-sized room. On one wall was what looked like a workbench and on that workbench were two of the Green Goblin's jet-gliders, both dusted off and polished.

And on the wall above the bench hung Goblin costumes, Goblin gloves, and rows and rows of pumpkin bombs.

The man moved to the wall and took down the green and purple costume. He held up the mask, with its purple hat, long green ears, and diabolical grin. Just looking at it made the man shudder with slight fear and much respect. Norman Osborn had been a genius, of that there was no doubt.

He laid the mask on the bench and picked the purple sparkle-beam shooting gloves off the wall and placed them beside the mask. Sparkle-beams were blasts of pure energy that could blow a hole through a wall. Both gloves, when fully charged, could fire those beams almost as fast as machine guns fired bullets.

The arms and legs of the main costume were made of a green stretch material. He started to slip it on. The man from Chicago had no supply of Stromm's serum and probably wouldn't have taken it if he had. He figured that with enough work he could master everything, including the glider. What was important was that the person who wore the costume became the Goblin.

"Time to practice killing a Spider-Man," he said, and his voice echoed through the empty room as he pulled on the green and purple costume.

"I can't think of anything more fun."

Whistling, he pulled the mask over his face and became the Green Goblin.

\* \* \*

Winter had already arrived in the high mountains of Colorado. The wind swirled the light flakes and moaned through the pine trees. Two inches of snow had covered the forest floor the night before and tonight it was snowing again around the small three-room log cabin.

Inside, a fire in the stone fireplace cast an orange glow over the sparse furnishings, fighting the white light from an overhead fixture above a wooden table.

The table was covered with the remains of four TV dinners and a dozen rolled-up maps. Three men sat at the table silently watching a fourth man pace and talk on the phone. The man on the phone was named Richard Lee. He was the person in charge.

Even though the room was warm Lee kept a light windbreaker zipped up under his chin. He also wore a thin leather glove on his left hand. The other three men at the table had never seen him without that glove on. And none had dared ask why.

After a very short conversation, Lee hung up the phone and turned to the three men. "We have the go ahead," he said without a smile. "Head down the hill and prepare your teams. Tomorrow night by this time we will all be very, very rich."

The other three men nodded and stood without saying a word. The plans were made. They all knew what they had to do. One by one they silently filed into the snow-filled night and cold mountain air.

There was nothing left to say.

# CHAPTER (3)

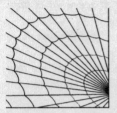 Peter had managed to get home without seeing any other ghosts of dead foes. But he had looked for them in every face and in every window and door.

Mary Jane had fed him a part of a sandwich and a glass of milk. By the time she had helped him to the bedroom and pulled the covers up around his chin he was sound asleep. Mary Jane had pulled the curtain to shut out the light and then tiptoed from the room.

And for a short time the dreams and nightmares left Peter alone.

But for only a short time.

Then they started.

\* \* \*

*Peter is standing in front of Norman Osborn's big desk in the Osborn building. The light coming through the windows seems extra bright and Peter wants to shade his eyes, but can't. His hands and arms won't move from his sides. Peter is young, only in his teens.*

*Norman Osborn sits at his desk lecturing Peter about something. But Peter can't hear him. Osborn's mouth is moving, but no sounds come out.*

*The light from the huge windows behind Osborn keeps getting brighter and brighter as he talks without sound.*

*Straining to look into the light, Peter can see the silhouette of Osborn's head in front of the window. Osborn's head seems to be changing shape, his ears growing, his* jaw getting longer, as Peter strains to see what is happening.

Then, just as Peter can't stand the light for one more second, Osborn starts laughing.

At first Peter can't hear the laugh, but he can see that Osborn has his head back and is obviously laughing long and hard.

"It must be funny," Peter tries to say, but no sound comes out of his mouth either.

Soon Peter can hear Osborn's laugh—the high, hysterical cackle of the Green Goblin. And the laugh is more painful than the bright light.

As Peter fights against whatever is holding him in place, the light fades and Norman Osborn turns into the Green Goblin. The desk and chair morph into a goblin-glider.

Peter becomes Spider-Man as the Green Goblin flies out the window directly into the light, laughing all the way.

Spider-Man can now move and he tries to follow, but can't get past the window. The light seems to stop him right at the edge of the building. He can't go up or down. He claws at the invisible barrier that won't let him chase his enemy.

Suddenly Spider-Man hears a familiar voice behind him. He is older now. Late teens, early twenties. He feels much older than his real age.

"Peter, why did you let me die?"

Spider-Man turns around to see Gwen Stacy standing in the doorway facing him.

"Spider-Man, I hate you!" Gwen shouts.

Then she says calmly, "Peter, why did you let me die?"

46

"Gwen—?" Spidey says. Around them Osborn's office walls dissolve until Spidey and Gwen are standing on the top of the stone pillar of the Brooklyn Bridge.

Peter can feel the wind, and smell the city and the water. Above them the Green Goblin circles on his glider. He is laughing and the laugh cuts at Spider-Man, making him cover his ears.

As if in slow motion, the Green Goblin swoops in and knocks Gwen from the top of the bridge.

Spidey moves to catch her, but it feels as if his legs are plastered in wet cement.

She falls.

He fights to move, to catch her, to save her from falling to her death in the water below.

Finally he reaches the edge of the stone and looks down.

She falls.

He shoots a web after her and catches her.

She is still dead. The fall has killed her.

Then the nightmare gets worse as Gwen dies over and over and over above that river, like an old phonograph with the needle stuck.

Finally, with one final forever-scream from Gwen, the scene shifts to an alley.

Spider-Man pulls the Green Goblin from his glider and it comes around and crushes the Goblin against the wall.

Norman Osborn is dead.

The Green Goblin is dead.

It happens so fast and then it is replayed faster and faster and faster.

Spidey leans over the body as the face of Norman

*changes to Harry and then the Hobgoblin and then back to Norman.*

*And then suddenly Spider-Man is back on top of the bridge and Gwen is falling toward the river and the river has become a floating mass of dead bodies. And the streets of the city are filled with bodies.*

*Then the bodies become a river of blood.*

*The blood flows everywhere.*

*Gwen falls toward the blood.*

*A face forms in the blood. A face with a huge mouth and razor-pointed teeth, and Gwen is falling directly into the mouth and Spider-Man can't stop her fall.*

*He shoots a web to catch her, but his web is a stream of blood that only covers her.*

*The blood flows.*

*Gwen falls.*

*Then Gwen looks up at where Spider-Man is standing on top of the bridge, and her face changes into the face of Mary Jane as a huge tongue of blood laps up and surrounds her.*

*"Peter!" Mary Jane's face seems to say as the tongue of blood takes her. "Why did you let me die? I loved you. Why did you let me die?"*

*"No!" Spider-Man screams. Blood drips from his hands and his fingers and his web-shooters.*

*Norman Osborn's blood.*

*Harry Osborn's blood.*

*Uncle Ben's blood.*

*Gwen's blood.*

*Mary Jane's blood.*

*The blood of the city.*

48

\* \* \*

"Peter! Wake up!"

The voice was distant, but it got through. Peter fought out of the nightmare of blood and death. An overwhelming feeling of relief flooded him as he realized it was just another nightmare.

Mary Jane was holding him.

He took a deep, shuddering breath.

"A nightmare?" he asked softly.

"Must have been a bad one," Mary Jane said, hugging him. He was covered in sweat and the blankets and sheets were off the bed. Mary Jane looked as if she had been through a pretty good wrestling match getting him to wake up.

"You all right?" he asked her. "I didn't hurt you, did I?" He was always afraid his strength would harm her.

She shook her head no. "I'm fine. Are you?"

"Worse this time," he said. The sun still lit the window. The clock on the bed stand told Peter he had been asleep for an hour.

A very long hour.

Peter shivered and then looked up into the eyes of Mary Jane. He could tell she was worried. He hugged her. "Thanks for waking me up."

She laughed. "You were tearing the place apart. I had to."

Peter looked down at the tangled pile of blankets and sheets. "Thanks."

"You want to try getting a little more sleep?"

The thought of Mary Jane falling into that huge mouth

in the river of blood made Peter shudder. Mary Jane held him tight and after a moment he relaxed.

"Maybe a little later," he said. "I've got another idea." He pulled her face down over his and kissed her hard and long.

After a moment she kissed him back equally as hard.

It turned out that Mary Jane liked his other idea.

\* \* \*

An hour later Peter sat alone at the kitchen table, slowly munching on the remainder of his sandwich and drinking a glass of milk. Mary Jane was taking a nap, but he'd been afraid to let himself drift back to sleep beside her. At least not before he gave that last nightmare some thought. But he was so tired he couldn't hold a thought long enough to make sense of anything.

He slid a notepad Mary Jane used for grocery lists in front of him and wrote a number *1* at the top. Beside the number he wrote: *I'm exhausted.*

"Boy is that an understatement," he said aloud.

Beside the number *2* he wrote: *Worried about the serum, who has it, and what they will do with the serum.*

Beside a number *3* he wrote: *Feel responsible for the vial being stolen.*

"Now isn't that interesting," Peter said. He leaned back and took another bite of the sandwich as he stared at the paper. He knew the theft of the vial was driving him, but until he wrote down number three he didn't completely realize he felt responsible for its theft. He had never blamed Reed, but he hadn't realized he was blaming himself.

He thought back over other crimes he felt responsible

for. As always, he came back to the death of his Uncle Ben soon after he first became Spider-Man.

The day his Uncle Ben died was with him as if it was yesterday. A few weeks before Uncle Ben was killed, Peter had been accidentally bitten by a radioactive spider while attending a science demonstration in high school.

Soon after, he had figured out what had happened and had discovered some of his new powers. But his ego had let him think he could now do anything, that the power had no responsibility with it.

But he had been so wrong.

Power always carried a vast amount of responsibility.

The day Ben died, Peter had just come from an interview where he was going to make a lot of money and be very famous, or so he thought. As he came out of the building, a robber was chased past him by police. It would have been nothing for Spider-Man to stop the robber and help the cops. But Peter, as Spider-Man, felt he was too good for such petty things.

That night he discovered that his Uncle Ben had been killed by a robber, the same one he could have stopped and put in jail earlier that day. From that moment onward he knew the true responsibility that came with his special powers.

And he never forgot.

But looking back, Peter knew, without a doubt, that he had been responsible for Uncle Ben's death. He had used that feeling of responsibility to keep pushing him to become the Spider-Man he was today.

He took a long drink of milk and stared at the paper. He felt responsible for Gwen Stacy's death. She had been his girlfriend and the Green Goblin had known that fact and used it against Spider-Man. Being around him had put her in extreme danger and had eventually gotten her killed. Just like Uncle Ben's, there was little doubt he was responsible for her death, even though the Green Goblin had been the one who actually pushed her from the Brooklyn Bridge. It didn't matter. She would not have been on that bridge if not for Spider-Man.

So how many other deaths did he feel responsible for? Norman Osborn? Harry Osborn? Kraven the Hunter? Ned Leeds? Every person killed by Venom and Carnage? His tired mind wouldn't let him think about it much beyond that point. That way lay true madness.

He finished off the sandwich and slid the plate to the center of the table. Then he marked a number *4* on the sheet. Beside that he wrote: *I am having nightmares.*

"No kidding," he said. He stared at the sheet for a moment, but nothing came to mind beyond the unknown face in the river of blood. Besides, what help could a nightmare be to him?

He wrote a number *5* on the paper followed by: *I am obsessed with finding the serum.*

"Getting all the obvious ones," he said. He drew a line linking number one and number five. Then another line along the side to link the other three with one and five.

He finished off the milk and sat staring at his short list. After a few minutes more of staring at the sheet he finally said to himself, *This isn't getting me anywhere. Maybe if I go take some photos I can tame this obsession.*

He suddenly felt better, as if making a decision and dealing with more everyday types of things had given him a new burst of energy. He quickly crumpled up his list and stuck it in his pocket. Then on a fresh piece of paper he left a note for Mary Jane saying he was going down to the *Daily Bugle* and that he would bring home dinner.

Feeling lighter than he had in days, he went out the front door and headed for the subway.

# CHAPTER 4

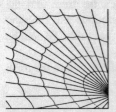The Colorado weather was being nice to Richard Lee, much more than he ever could have hoped for, or expected. A light snow drifted from the sky almost like a child's imaginary Christmas Eve. Just enough snow to cover the upcoming operation, but not enough to get in their way. The temperature hovered around the mid-twenties, not too cold. Perfect for what he was planning.

Lee, a solidly built redhead, took off his night goggles and checked his watch one more time. Less than a minute until it started. He blew the flakes of snow off the lens of his binoculars and checked out the well-lit building in the clearing.

The Vault, a high security prison for super-villain types, sat in the middle of a five-acre, empty field carved out of the middle of an old pine forest. A helicopter pad filled one corner of the field, and the only road inside was on the opposite side from Lee. The rest of the field looked like nothing more than close-cut weeds slowly being covered by a thin layer of snow. Actually, between the trees and the fence was a very deadly mine field.

As with more normal prisons, the Vault was designed to keep its "guests" inside, not to withstand an assault from the outside. Even the mine field was designed to stop anyone who got out through the fence from making it to the trees.

But tonight the Vault was going to get a full-scale assault from outside and behind.

Lee studied the high fence, the guard towers on the four

corners, and the mined area between the trees and the fence. He knew every inch of the grounds and building by heart. In five minutes they would be inside. Of that he had no doubt at all.

Lee glanced at his watch, then said firmly into the mike attached to his helmet, "Time. Let's do it."

"Roger that," Ellison said in Lee's ear.

"Copy," Harken said.

"On our way," Davis said.

Lee stood and stepped out of the cover of large trees so he could see the movement of his men.

It took a moment, but then fifty men separated from the trees and the surrounding bushes and started slowly across the field through the light snow. Ellison was in charge of ten men on the far right. He would be the first through the fence when the time came. Harken and his men had the big gun. Actually it was an Army antitank weapon Harken had mounted on a big tripod. He had altered it to fire a larger rocket with a heavier charge. Everyone just called it the big gun.

Davis had the rest of the men under his command. He would be in charge of the assault on the actual cells inside. Half his men carried enough explosives to level any normal building. They'd need the explosives to get through cell doors, and even walls if necessary.

Lee watched through the light snow as the men moved forward slowly, clearly in no hurry. As they moved, a low, almost rumbling sound came from behind them. Suddenly over them were two black silhouettes against the snow-filled sky.

Lee smiled to himself and noted the time. Right on the money. Two silenced choppers moved over the trees, their normal engine sound muffled by almost a thousand times, their skins had been painted pure black to blend them into the night sky—it backfired slightly, what with the snow, but still, they were barely visible. After a moment they were in position in front of the men in the meadow.

Lee knew the choppers were stolen Russian choppers, altered for his purpose. They'd been flown in from Greenland and down through Canada, never getting far enough above the ground to alert government radar. It had been a long and expensive operation to get them here, but it was going to be worth it tonight.

The two helicopters, moving almost as one, started slowly toward the Vault. A very wide, reddish beam shot out of the belly of each and moved slowly over the open field. After a short moment the first explosion rang out as a buried mine was detonated.

"Here we go," Lee said into his mike. "Everyone stay alert."

Soon more explosions followed as if a string of firecrackers was going off.

Lee nodded and watched as the helicopters slowly cleared the mine field.

The Vault's two main defenses from outside attacks were the mine fields and the high wire fence guarded by the four towers. After the helicopters finished setting off the mines, the mine field would be a useless mass of loose dirt and holes. The worst thing that could happen to someone in that field would be to fall in a hole and break a leg.

Lee turned to his left and watched as Harken and two men set up the large gun just on the edge of the mine field. Two other men came up lugging one shell each, followed close behind by two others, each carrying another shell.

As the two helicopters reached the halfway point of the field, high, wailing sirens from the Vault suddenly mixed with the explosions from the mines and the low rumble of the choppers. After a moment large searchlights shot out from the guard towers and the building behind it, sending bright beams across the field at his men.

*Three seconds late*, Lee noted. *Maybe we caught them with the second shift on duty.*

The dust and debris from the mine explosions and the falling snow blocked the view of the camouflaged men moving slowly across the now safe mine field. Lee nodded to himself. Again everything was perfect.

The helicopters finished their pass over the mine field and swung quickly off over the trees where they would wait for the evacuation. Lee turned to Harken and the big gun. "Blow them out of there," he said.

Harken nodded and said, "Fire."

Lee's ears were protected by both a helmet and earphones, but the explosion from the big gun still left a ringing sound. That little thing was one loud and powerful weapon.

The guard tower on the left disintegrated in a second huge explosion. A good fifty feet of fence on both sides was peeled back like someone opening a large can. Bodies of the Vault's Guardsmen flew like toys through the night air. Harken hadn't lied when he had told Lee not to worry about the gun doing its job.

The men around the gun quickly reloaded with a practiced and smooth motion. Lee nodded in satisfaction. Harken just might earn a good bonus on this after all.

A moment later the tower on the right corner of the fence around the Vault disintegrated. Fifteen seconds later, the far tower. The fourth tower was out of sight beyond the main building, near the road's entrance, so there was no need to knock it down.

In his headphones Lee heard Davis give the next order to his men. "Double-time. Get into position."

As a unit, the men around Davis moved up to the edge of the mine field and dropped into positions, weapons aimed at the brightly lit side of the Vault.

Ellison and his ten men moved in through the left opening in the high security fence. Gunfire opened up at them from a position about halfway up the Vault's wall.

Davis's men quickly returned fire, efficiently silencing the defender. Within a few seconds Ellison had his men in position.

A small explosion opened a hole in the side of the main building. Then Ellison's men spread out, taking up defense positions around the opening as Davis and his men moved in. Lee glanced at his watch. Right on the money. Not a hitch.

Lee moved along behind Davis and his men, staying low and watching everything. The men poured inside the Vault, easily taking care of what little resistance they met. From this point to the main cells it would be an easy fight. Getting in had been the hard part and that had gone like a cakewalk.

Lee moved through the destroyed security fence and up to Ellison. Ellison nodded and gave Lee a thumbs-up sign as he approached.

Lee nodded to Ellison and spoke into his mike. "Davis, your status?"

"Passage secured to the designated area," Davis said in Lee's ear.

"Hold there," Lee said. "I'm on my way."

Davis and his men knew where they were heading inside the building. They just didn't know why. The why and the who they were rescuing was only Lee's business. And the man who had hired him. Lee smiled as he ducked through the new, wide opening in the side of the Vault and moved toward the cells. Soon the job would be done and he would be very, very rich. They all would. The easiest retirement money he had ever dreamed of having.

\* \* \*

Peter let the sounds of the active city street outside the *Daily Bugle* wash over him. It was lunch hour and everyone on the sidewalk seemed so alive and healthy. Not a drop of blood in sight. And no ghosts, either. Peter let the fall sun warm him and the feeling of the crowd calm him.

There was just something special about New York that couldn't really be found anywhere else. Standing on a busy sidewalk in this city made a person feel alive and part of something much bigger, something that had much more energy. That energy seemed to fill the people who visited, sending them home feeling as if they'd lived more simply by going to New York. Those who lived in the city felt they were just a little more special than anyone who lived in the rest of the world. For many New Yorkers, anything that happened outside the city really didn't matter. New York had the best food. The best shopping. The best everything. For most New Yorkers, the world started and ended with the city.

And in many ways it was all true. A full world of things

could be found inside the city, so what was the point of going anywhere else? Peter knew deep down that he was one of those New York snobs. He loved the city, and at the moment he was letting it fill him with much needed energy.

"Parker!" The deep voice cut through the energy of the city and spun Peter around. J. Jonah Jameson, the publisher of the *Bugle* and Peter's boss was barreling down on him like a bull after a red flag.

"Oh, oh," Peter said. "Time to pay the piper."

Jonah had a large cigar stuck in his mouth and his perpetual scowl on his face. He was a thick-shouldered man who seemed much taller than his actual height. He had just come out of his limo and, like Peter, was heading to the entrance of the *Bugle* building.

It had been two weeks since Peter had even stopped into the *Bugle* newsroom. Jameson was probably going to tear him apart.

Jonah's big hand reached out and grabbed Peter by the shoulder. Peter flinched, but didn't step back.

"Glad to see you up and around," Jonah said gruffly, patting Peter on the back hard enough to make Peter cough. "From what that wife of yours has been telling us, you really had a pretty nasty flu bug."

"Still pretty tired," Peter managed to stammer out. So Mary Jane had been fielding assignment calls from the *Bugle* while he concentrated on finding the stolen vial. He loved that woman more and more every day.

Jonah looked him right in the eye. "But obviously you're okay now, so I assume I'll be seeing front-page photos from . . ."

Jonah trailed off, and his eyes suddenly grew wide as

he stared at something behind Peter. Finally he stammered, ''What the—?''

Peter broke out of Jonah's grip and turned. It took him only a moment to see what Jonah had seen. Norman Osborn was strolling down the other side of the street just as plain as day. He moved in and around other people on the sidewalk like a native New Yorker. He was clearly no ghost.

Simultaneously Jonah and Peter both started across the street after Norman Osborn. Or Osborn's twin. Or his ghost. Whoever it was.

Osborn, not seeming to notice the two men approaching him, turned into the entrance to a busy department store and disappeared into the crowd going through the open doors.

Both Peter and Jonah shoved people aside as they fought their way through the crowd until they too were inside.

A huge sign hung from the ceiling proclaiming the ''Fall Sale.'' The main area of the store was huge, with wide tile floors and islands holding merchandise. A mezzanine circled the main floor, with merchandise on one side and a restaurant on the other. From just inside the door Peter could see hundreds of people.

The guy who looked like Norman Osborn shouldn't have been more than twenty yards ahead of them, going down one of the aisles between the merchandise. But he was nowhere to be seen.

Peter stopped cold, letting the crowd move around him. Standing on tiptoes, he scanned the crowd.

Jonah went on another few steps before stopping and

doing the same. After a long minute he turned and moved back to Peter.

"You saw Norman Osborn?" Jonah asked.

Peter nodded. "More likely someone who looked just like him."

Jonah shook his head and looked around the crowded entry to the department store. "No. I *know* Norman Osborn when I see him and that was him."

"Don't you think that might be tough," Peter said, "considering he's been dead for years?"

Jonah made a motion as if brushing aside a fly. "I always thought old Norman was too crafty to be killed. I bet he just faked his death and now that his son Harry is gone, he's come back to reclaim what's left of his business. What a scoop this will make."

Jonah turned and grabbed both of Peter's shoulders. "Get me a picture of Norman Osborn. Any way you can."

"But . . ."

"What a scoop," Jonah said again, turning and heading almost at a run for the front door of the store.

With his mouth open, standing in the middle of the crowd, Peter stood watching his boss's back.

He'd watched Norman Osborn, as the original Green Goblin, get killed as his own glider pinned him against a brick wall. Peter could understand if another Green Goblin showed up. Harry and the Hobgoblin had proven that was very, very possible. Norman and Harry must have spent half their time building secret rooms for Goblin equipment.

But another Norman Osborn? That wasn't so possible.

Peter scanned the busy shoppers. There had to be another answer. There just had to be.

* * *

The cool wind was blowing the last of the leaves off the rooftop patio trees as Bogal stood, hands on hips, staring out over the city. His blue suit and blue tie were in sharp contrast to the gray of the building stone and the gray fall sky.

All his men were trained and in place on twenty-five different buildings scattered around the area. From where Bogal stood he could see five different teams. All were in readiness. He had spent the morning checking them all.

Soon the vial would be back in the laboratories of Lifestream Technologies and out of the dangerous hands of that maverick web-spinner. And Bogal would be rich.

"Okay, Spider-Man," Bogal said to the city below. "Come to me."

# CHAPTER 5

Richard Lee strode down the cement and steel-lined hallway, moving past a few cell doors until he reached a specific one. He'd had to step over the armored bodies of five Vault Guardsmen. Ellison's team had been equipped with a device called a "screamer," which, when activated, rendered the Guardsmen's high-tech armor useless.

So far it seemed Lee hadn't lost a man. He hoped that would be the case through the entire mission, even though he had made plans on carrying away at least a dozen bodies of his own men.

A number 6 was stenciled on the door he faced, and a computer punchboard embedded in the concrete served as a lock. A sign above the lock warned of high voltage.

He pointed at the door. "Get it open."

Davis and three other men stepped forward, pulling out equipment and explosives.

"There will be two armed Guardsmen on the other side of that door," Lee said to Davis. "And two more in an inner cell."

Davis nodded as Lee stepped back down the hall out of the line of fire. With quick work, Davis and his men set three small charges. "Now," Davis said and all three men stepped quickly back.

The explosions sent a small shock wave down the narrow hall, and Lee had to catch himself against a wall. A cloud of concrete dust billowed through the air. Davis and his men, weapons firing blindly ahead of them, moved quickly into the dust.

A few blasts of return fire answered and then were silent. A few more seconds passed before Lee heard Davis's voice in his earphone. "Outer cell clear. We are—"

Lee had started for the cell door when Davis's voice stopped. "Davis, report!"

"Sir," Davis said after only a second. "Do you know whose cell this is?"

Lee nodded, letting a small smile cross his face. Now he understood why Davis had stopped talking. Davis had looked through the window between the two parts of the cell at the prisoner and had recognized who it was.

Quickly, Lee ducked through the ruined door and stepped over one Guardsman's body. Four men and Davis were standing at the bulletproof window staring at the prisoner and two Guardsmen crouched at ready. The Guardsmen had their gauntlets pointed at the window, even though they all knew that no one was coming through the bulletproof glass.

The prisoner stood inside a shimmering blue field of electricity, on a platform in the very center of the cell. He too was facing the window, smiling.

The interior cell beyond the window was the size of a small half-court basketball gym, with concrete floors and block walls. In the very center of the floor was a platform raised about two feet. A bed, a chair, a sink, and a toilet were the only items on the platform. The faintly blue, shimmering electric shield went from floor to the high ceiling around the platform. Lee also knew from his study of this cell that the field extended below the platform and above through the ceiling. The controls were here in the outer cell, but it took a very special code to shut it down. They would free the prisoner another way.

# GOBLIN'S REVENGE

The prisoner, Cletus Kasady, stood inside the electric shield beside the chair, facing the window, a half-amused expression on his face. He was tall, almost bone thin, with red hair and pale skin. He didn't look like much at all, but Lee knew better. That man, under that weak-looking exterior, was Carnage, the worst serial killer of all time.

Lee stared at the prisoner and the prisoner stared back.

Someone was paying a vast amount of money to free this killer. When it came to that much money Lee didn't ask why. He just did his job and kept his mouth shut.

"Break him out of there," Lee said.

Davis looked up at him, his face white from cement dust and his eyes wide with fear. "Sir, that man is Carnage."

Lee nodded. "I am fully aware of that. Carnage is the point of this entire mission. We're here to rescue him."

"Sir, I—"

"Complete the mission," Lee said turning back to the window and Kasady. "Get him out of there."

"I can't do that," Davis said. "He would—"

Lee turned and with a quick burst from his machine gun cut Davis in half, splattering blood and intestines on the window and two of his men beside him. Then he turned and faced the other men in the room, gun still at ready. "Now, does anyone else have an objection to finishing this mission and getting out of here alive?"

All four men shook their heads "no" while staring at Davis's still-twitching body.

"Good," Lee said, pointing the muzzle of his machine gun at the door. "Then kill those two guards and get Kasady out of there."

Through the glass Kasady silently laughed and Lee nodded in his direction.

Then Lee turned his back on the window and spoke into his chin microphone. "Helicopters, stand by for evacuation. I need three more men inside at once."

As he talked, two of Davis's men wired the door with explosives. Beyond the window Lee could see the two remaining Vault Guardsmen take up positions facing the door, gauntlets ready. They were facing their deaths and they knew it, but there seemed to be no hesitation on their part. Their job was to guard Carnage and they were trained to do just that. That level of devotion always impressed Lee. It was too bad they had to die.

Three more men came in through the door and hesitated when they saw Davis's body. Lee waved them into positions against the walls.

"Ready," one man said as he finished placing the last device on the door and stepped back. Two men were flat on their stomachs facing the door. The others had guns at ready.

"Blow it," Lee said.

Again the explosions sent a cloud of dust billowing through the room as the metal interior door was slammed inward. When the explosion opened the door the two men on the floor sprayed the inside Vault Guardsmen through the dust, cutting them both down almost without a fight.

Lee nodded. His men had been trained well. They would all get a bonus. He stepped over Davis's body and moved through the swirling dust to the inside cell.

Kasady stood inside the blue, high-voltage walls, smiling at Lee. "Are you my white knight?"

Lee shrugged. "Just the hired hand, here to return you

to the outside world.'' Lee turned to his men through the still swirling dust. "Cut this electric shield.''

"But, sir . . .'' One man started to say.

Lee swung around, machine gun pointed at the man's middle. He hadn't expected this much trouble from his own men. He had expected some, which was why their actual objective had been kept secret until this point. "You want a bonus?" Lee said, smiling. "Or what Davis got?"

The man took a step back, his face white. He glanced up at the smiling Kasady inside the blue shimmering shield and then back at Lee. Then he nodded to two other men and they moved forward to the base of the platform. They set five small explosive charges equidistant around the base and then stepped back.

"Ready,'' he told Lee.

Lee turned to Kasady. "Stay directly in the middle and you won't be hurt.''

Kasady just nodded.

"Do it,'' Lee said.

The explosion this time was much smaller, but the cloud of dust filled the air, blocking all sight of the platform. Lee looked up near the ceiling, above the cloud of dust and watched as the blue electric shield around the platform flickered once and then went off.

Lee nodded and stepped toward the edge of the platform. But before he could take a second step Kasady appeared out of the dust.

Then Kasady scratched his cheek with a single fingernail. Blood started to seep from the cut.

No, Lee realized, the blood didn't seep, it *moved*. And it could not have been real blood, as real blood wasn't this solid. Nor did real blood expand to cover one's entire body.

Lee had seen pictures of Carnage, but they had not prepared him for facing the real thing face to face. No sign of Kasady was left. The man's thin body had been transformed into a huge, rippling-muscled creature. The eyes had become white pools and the huge mouth was full of pointed, razor teeth.

The skin of the monster had become red, with constantly swirling black patterns forming and then changing. Parts of the skin seemed to drip off, reforming with the main body. His fingers had become long, thin razor claws, with nails that curled into needlepoint tips.

Lee's men all staggered back, guns up and ready. But before they could even get a shot off spikes formed on Carnage's arm and shot out like a fan opening on a hot day. They sliced bloody holes in each man's head, splattering blood all over the walls.

Carnage took a step toward Lee, reached out with an arm that seemed to grow in length as it went, and picked Lee up. Lee didn't struggle. He knew enough about Carnage to know that struggling would only get him killed.

"Tell me, hired gun," Carnage said, holding Lee very close to the razor teeth. Carnage's breath smelled like a body left to rot in the sun, and all Lee could stare at was the swirling of the razor teeth. "Who sent you?"

Lee shook his head from side to side for a moment before he managed to choke out, "I don't know."

Carnage's grip tightened on Lee's shirt as he pulled him even closer to that huge mouth. "How could you not know?"

The smell of Carnage's breath almost caused Lee to

pass out, but he managed to hold on. He was just glad it had been some time since breakfast. "Hired over—phone," Lee choked out. "Paid—through Swiss accounts."

Carnage nodded and dropped Lee to the floor. Lee rolled over and stared up at Carnage as he walked around the platform without climbing back on it, obviously thinking.

He reached Lee again and stood over him. "Freeing me makes no sense."

Lee shrugged. "I was just paid to do a job and I've done it," Lee said. "I have two helicopters waiting outside to take you away from here, if that is what you'd like."

"And how many more men?"

"Forty-five," Lee said, "plus pilots."

Carnage laughed, wringing his hands together as if he were a starving man sitting over a turkey dinner. "Oh, this will be so much fun."

Carnage reached down and pulled Lee off the floor like an adult picking up a rag doll left behind by a child. "I suppose I should be grateful to you," Carnage said. Carnage pulled him close and stared into Lee's eyes. "Well, should I? You tell me."

"No need," Lee managed to say.

Carnage nodded. "Good. Because I have a Spider-Man to kill and I hate being grateful to anyone."

Carnage laughed, choking Lee with the smell of death and rot. Then Carnage held Lee out at arm's length. "But as my way of saying thanks, I will kill you slowly."

Before Lee even realized what Carnage had said small knives formed on his body and flicked out, cutting at Lee.

"The old skin game," Carnage said.

Lee glanced down and saw the skin on both his arms peeled back.

"Don't you just love games?" Carnage said, laughing. Before Lee passed out from the pain the swirling knives from Carnage started cutting off the skin on his chest, working down.

*   *   *

The sound from the *Daily Bugle*'s newsroom washed over Peter like a warm shower. He stood in the main double door and stared out over the huge room filled with desks, computers, and people. Busy people. The deadline for the evening edition of the paper was only a half hour away, so everyone seemed hectic, slightly panicked, and very normal.

Peter looked around, seeing the newsroom from almost a fresh perspective since he had been away from it for two weeks. Small paths wound in and out of the desks and file cabinets without any pattern. Along the far wall were five glass offices with all their doors wide open. The biggest of the glass offices was Jonah's and he and three others were in there having one of the continuous meetings that went on all day around a newspaper. Peter had sat in on more of those meetings over the years than he wanted to think about.

Peter took a deep breath of the air and let the smell of ink and newsprint wash over him. Until that moment he hadn't realized how much he had missed coming in here.

Peter watched as Jonah used his hands to emphasize a point he must have been making. After he had left Peter with the assignment to get a picture of Osborn, Peter had gone home. There he found a note from Mary Jane saying she would be back in an hour or so and he should fix himself something to eat. He had puttered around the apartment for a few minutes before finally getting up the courage to lie down on the couch.

The nap hadn't gone any better than any other sleep time over the past two weeks. He again had the nightmare of the river of blood filling the streets, but this time Norman Osborn's face formed in the blood. And then out of the blood flew fifty Green Goblins, all covered in blood and laughing. And as they attacked him Peter woke up sweating.

Peter let the image in his mind of the river of blood be pushed back by the very much alive feeling of the newsroom. He'd have to come in here more often, just to keep himself grounded in reality. And maybe to make some money.

He and Mary Jane could sure use almost any money at the moment. But he knew he wasn't going to do it by taking a picture of Norman Osborn. Norman was dead and had been for years. But Peter might get a picture of the guy who looked like him. That would make him some money and clear one thing from his mind.

Who stole the serum was another matter all together.

All the national and international news service teletypes were against the far wall. Their constant chatter was a background feature of the newsroom. As a reporter or photographer, you never noticed their constant sound. It was just part of the workplace. They ran pretty much twenty-four hours a day, pouring out a steady stream of paper and noise.

So when they all beeped and stopped at the same moment, everyone noticed.

Every head in the room snapped toward the old-style teletypes, and the meeting in Jonah's office stopped just as suddenly. Jonah moved quickly to the door, staring at the machines. Nothing stopped those teletypes, or even made them pause for long except a major news flash being reported almost simultaneously by all the news sources. The beeps indicated that was happening.

It seemed as if everyone in the room was holding their breath, faces turned toward the teletypes. It took only a short moment before all of the machines burst back into life. Three of the closest reporters jumped toward them, suddenly unfrozen by the sound. Sandy Pines, a young blond-haired kid reached them first.

Sandy bent over the UP machine, studying the type coming off the teletype. "Wow!" he said, then turned and announced to the waiting room. "Someone broke into the Vault in Colorado and sprang Carnage."

Peter felt his stomach twist up into a tiny knot and his tired legs go numb under him. He leaned against a nearby desk and took a few deep breaths. Around him the newsroom burst into an explosion of activity.

Jonah screamed to three reporters at desks near his office. "Pull the front page." All three scrambled as if death itself was after them.

"Parker!" Jonah bellowed, his voice cutting across the madhouse the newsroom had just become. "Get me your best file photo of Carnage and three others for inside shots."

Peter raised his hand indicating he had heard and Jonah turned away, moving to the next detail. Peter stood and almost on automatic headed for the photo files contained in big cabinets in a room just off the newsroom.

The smaller room blocked some of the chaotic sound from the newsroom, but Peter didn't much notice. Like a zombie, he moved to the cabinet. His exhausted mind just couldn't grasp the thought that Carnage was free again. And most likely headed this way. It seemed that the nightmare with Dr. Catrall's serum just wouldn't stop. And Peter doubted he had the energy left to even give Carnage a fair fight.

Peter pulled out the file labeled "Carnage." He spread it open on a cluttered table in the center of the room.

Carnage's face stared back at him. Peter had taken a number of photos of Carnage with an automatic camera, usually while he and Carnage were fighting. The top photo in the file had caught Carnage in a fall, right after Spider-Man had knocked him off a building. Carnage was snarling and drool was flying from his mouth.

The very existence of Carnage had indirectly been Peter's fault.

While fighting on a distant planet, Peter had found what he thought was a great new costume. It formed around him when he wanted it to and seemed to give him extra powers. So Peter brought it back to Earth with him. But when he discovered that the costume was a symbiote and that it was about to join permanently with Peter, Peter got rid of it, thinking he had killed it.

But the spurned symbiote was angry at him and very much alive. Filled with revenge, the symbiote joined with an embittered, insane man to become Venom. Then one day, while breaking out of jail, Venom left a small drop of his symbiote on the edge of a hole in the wall of a jail cell.

The other occupant of that jail cell just happened to be Cletus Kasady, a notorious serial killer. Kasady's theory of life was that chaos should rule. When he and the drop of symbiote left by Venom joined, they formed a new creature, one bent on killing and creating chaos everywhere they went. They became Carnage, the worst and most powerful cold-blooded killer the world has ever seen.

Peter glanced at the pictures and then pulled one aside. Quickly he flipped through others, remembering each fight, pulling the pictures he knew Jonah would use. He had long ago stopped blaming himself for Carnage. But every so often, the thoughts came back. Especially when he was this tired.

The last few pictures in the folder had been taken two weeks before. They were pictures of Spider-Man fighting Carnage on the tower in Central Park.

Peter sighed. They had been battling for the control of Dr. Catrall's deadly serum. Spider-Man had won until someone stole the serum from Reed.

The image of the river of blood flowing between the buildings of New York filled Peter's mind before he could stop it. He slammed the file shut and put it back into the cabinet.

Outside the door to the photo room a young intern hurried by.

"Keating!" Peter yelled.

The intern stopped, a harried look on his face, then turned and came back to the photo room door. The kid, a dark-headed college freshman was on his way to becoming a damn fine reporter. But at the moment he was paying his dues by being an intern, the kid who got what someone else needed, including coffee and doughnuts.

"Glad to see you back, Peter," Keating said. "I'm sort of in a—"

Peter scooped up the pictures on the table and handed them to Keating. "Jonah needs these at once."

Keating started to object until he saw the subject of the photos. "On my way," he said, and with the pictures in one hand he turned and headed at a fast clip toward Jonah's office.

Walking like he was in slow motion in a speeded up world, Peter moved across and out of the newsroom and up the stairs, trying to get his mind to work.

He didn't really have a plan. He'd switch into Spider-Man and get home quickly. He needed to talk to Mary Jane for a few minutes and then call Reed Richards to see if he had any news. And he also had to tell Reed about the most recent sighting of Norman Osborn.

"Don't forget Carnage," Peter said aloud. "I'm going to need help." He'd ask for Reed's help in case Carnage came back to the city. Peter was much too tired to be proud. As worn out and tired as he was, Spider-Man was going to need all the help he could get.

Peter moved out onto the roof and headed for his normal place to change clothes behind some heating duct work. Suddenly his spider-sense went wild. Someone was watching him so he couldn't change.

Ambling slowly toward the edge of the roof, pretending to just be staring out over the city, he studied the nearby roofs. Two men in gray suits stood on the roof of the building across from the *Daily Bugle*. One wore what looked like a fighter-pilot's headset. The other had a pair of binoculars and was slowly scanning the surrounding area.

Peter turned and headed along the edge of the roof as if he was just taking a late afternoon stroll. On top of a building one block away he could see two more men, also dressed the same way.

And across from them were two others. By the time he did a circle around the roof of the *Daily Bugle* building he had spotted six different teams of men, all in gray suits, all studying the surrounding city.

Maybe the FBI had changed their ways of looking for him.

Peter laughed and headed for the stairs. "Maybe you're just making stuff up," Peter said out loud. "You really need some sleep. Who knows what those guys are up to? Maybe they work for the discount suit store down off Broadway."

He was about to head for the stairs when something else caught his attention. At first he thought it was just a large pigeon and his tired eyes had deceived him.

But then the picture came clear.

"No, please no," Peter said softly.

The Green Goblin was flying high over the city on a goblin-glider, making tight loops and dives as if fighting someone.

Peter started to pull off his shirt to slip into his Spider-Man costume when his spider-sense again went wild, reminding him of the men in suits watching.

"Another day," Peter said to the Green Goblin. "Whoever you are."

So, without being able to chase the Green Goblin, Peter

stood and watched as his old foe made a few banking corners, swooped low in behind a neighboring building and disappeared.

After ten minutes of waiting without the Goblin returning, Peter turned and headed for the stairs.

On the subway heading home he slumped in his seat and then dozed.

He dreamed of a river of blood flowing between the buildings of the city. And there were two faces in the river of blood.

Carnage and the Green Goblin.

# CHAPTER 6

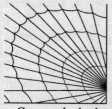 The light snowfall had stopped by the time Carnage appeared in the hole in the side of the Vault. But the ground around the jail was covered white, spotted only by a few bushes and camouflaged men.

Carnage had taken his time leaving the Vault, deciding to have some fun along the way. He'd searched out the barracks for the Guardsmen and had some fun killing a few he had come to know personally through his stay at the Vault. Since his unknown benefactor had given him the chance, he figured why not take the advantage? Who knew when he'd be in this neighborhood again?

But that fun was now done—it was time to find Spider-Man.

As Carnage stepped into the light snow a hail of gunfire opened up from the surrounding area. Ducking quickly to one side, he moved faster than the guns could track him until he finally had one of the soldiers by the uniform, holding him up as a shield to block more gunfire.

The shooting stopped instantly as the man in Carnage's hand kicked and squirmed. Carnage turned the guy around to face him and keep his back to his friends. "Why did you fire at me?"

The man choked for a moment, then managed to say, "I was ordered to."

"I'd say someone out here doesn't like me." Carnage looked around at all the men aiming rifles at him from positions in the snow. "So who gave the order?"

"Ellison," the man said, his voice high and squeaky. "Jeff Ellison."

"And if you point out this Ellison person, I just might let you live."

The man hanging in Carnage's grasp pointed in the direction of the ruined tower to the right. "The one with the golf cap."

A part of Carnage's skin formed into a saw and cut off the man's nose. The nose fell to the ground and blood spurted from the man's face in time with his pounding heart.

"Just in case you were lying, I didn't want your nose to grow on you." Carnage dropped him as the man started screaming.

The moment the man hit the ground the soldiers around the Vault again opened fire. But Carnage was much faster than they were.

Arrows formed on his arms and flew with deadly accuracy, cutting down every man shooting except the man with the golf cap. Suddenly, only the echoes of gunfire rang off the trees and snow-covered field.

"Mr. Ellison," Carnage said, sending out a tentacle and whipping Ellison's rifle from his hands. "You are a professional. I'm sure you will understand what I need to do."

Ellison stood, a look of horror on his face as he backed away.

Carnage advanced slowly toward him, smiling. Carnage's skin continually formed into weapons and then flowed back into his body, only to form into more instruments of death.

Ellison kept backing away, but there wasn't far he could go. After about ten feet he was flush against part of the security fence, his legs pushing to go farther, but the fence holding him tight.

Carnage moved right up into Ellison's face. "Do you know who paid to release me?"

Ellison shook his head "no."

"Are you sure?" Carnage said, leaning in even closer to Ellison's face.

With his head pushed back hard against the fence Ellison choked out, "I'm sure. Only Lee knew."

"The red-haired guy inside?"

Ellison managed to nod "yes."

"Well, he wasn't any help either," Carnage said. "He lost the old skin game."

Carnage leaned back, seeming to think, but Ellison remained pinned against the fence.

"I've decided," Carnage finally said. "Give me your hands."

Ellison started to extend his arms, his entire body shaking.

"No," Carnage said, "I wanted just your hands." With a quick action, razorlike knives formed on each of Carnage's arms and flashed out, slicing off Ellison's hands at the wrists.

Carnage caught the two hands and held them up in front of the shocked Ellison. "Now, that's what I was asking for. Better, don't you think?"

For a moment Ellison stared at the spurting stumps of his arms, then clutched them to his chest and slumped to the ground, still pressed against the fence. Blood soon stained his shirt and formed a red circle in the snow around him.

"Wave good-bye," Carnage said, using Ellison's hands

to wave at the Vault. "I will so miss this place. But I'm afraid I really can't stay. I have an appointment in New York with a Spider-Man."

He tossed the severed hands in the direction of his old cell. Then at a moderate walk, he headed downhill through the trees, whistling.

*  *  *

Mary Jane still wasn't home when Peter got there, so he paced for a short time, then laid down on the couch. And just as on the subway, he was so exhausted he dozed quickly.

And the dream came back.

*Thousands of bodies filling the streets. Dr. Catrall is standing on a building ledge next to Spider-Man. Both of them are staring at the vast streets filled with dead. Then Catrall turns to Spider-Man and says, "This is all your fault. You should have destroyed the serum."*

*And before Spidey can answer Catrall is gone and Spidey is standing on the top of the Brooklyn Bridge and Gwen Stacy, Peter's old girlfriend, is standing beside him. Below, the river is flowing red with blood.*

*"It's all your fault," Gwen says and as she does the Green Goblin, swooping out of nowhere, knocks her from the bridge.*

*The face in the river of blood forms below Gwen as she falls. The face of Carnage this time.*

*And as Spidey moves to try to save Gwen, Carnage's tendrils come up and covers her in blood.*

*Above Spider-Man the Green Goblin circles, laughing, taunting him that it is all his fault.*

And Peter woke up. He was sweating and the front door was opening.

\* \* \*

Mary Jane hadn't laughed so much in months.

She'd run into Flash Thompson while shopping. Flash was one of her and Peter's best friends from school. And then, after only a few minutes of talking with Flash, Liz Osborn, the widow of Harry Osborn came along.

Liz and her late husband had both been close to Peter and Mary Jane, though things had become strained around the time of Harry's death. The three of them had decided, right there in the vegetable aisle, that it had been way too long since they had spent time together.

They had decided to go get milkshakes and had ended up sitting and talking and laughing for over an hour. Mary Jane felt lighter and happier than she had in a long time. She knew Peter could use the same cheering up.

So she had invited both Liz and Flash over for dinner. "For old time's sake," she had said and Flash had told her that he wasn't that "old" yet.

As she unlocked the apartment and opened the door Peter swung around and sat up on the couch. He looked exhausted, with dark rings under his eyes. His hair was tussled and he was sweating. Mary Jane knew he must have just had another nightmare.

Peter frowned when he saw Flash and almost scowled when Liz came through the door, but Mary Jane pretended she didn't see his reaction. He needed some cheering up and this might just work.

"Wake up, sleepyhead," Mary Jane said, putting the sack of groceries on the table. "Company for dinner."

"Wow," Flash said, going over and dropping down on the couch next to Peter. "You look like death warmed over."

"Close," Peter said.

Mary Jane could tell Peter was in even a worse mood than this morning. But he needed some sort of distraction from his worry about that serum. Something to let him relax and then get some sleep.

"They must be keeping you going pretty hard at the paper, huh?" Flash said, ignoring Peter's short answer.

"Afraid so," Peter said. He stood. "Excuse me for a moment. I need to run some water over this head."

Peter moved off toward the back room as Flash looked up at Mary Jane with a puzzled look. After Peter closed the door Mary Jane said, "Sorry about that, Flash. Peter's just not sleeping that well lately."

Liz dropped her coat over the back of a chair and moved into the kitchen area beside Mary Jane. "I hope he isn't sick."

Mary Jane glanced at Liz. She had a deeply troubled look on her face, but Mary Jane couldn't quite read it.

"Not yet," Mary Jane said, squeezing Liz's arm and then turning to put the groceries together and start dinner. "Mostly just stress. And lack of sleep. But if it doesn't ease off it might turn into a health problem."

"So how do we unstress the guy?" Flash said, leaning against the counter and crossing his arms.

Mary Jane glanced at the closed bathroom door. "Good question. I think it—"

The bathroom door opened and Peter walked out. "Good seeing you guys, but I really need to get back to the paper. Hope you don't mind if I miss dinner."

"Peter?" Mary Jane said, taking a step toward him and then stopping. She knew that look in his eyes. There was no changing his mind.

"Going to miss your favorite," Flash said, his voice happy and light. "Sure work can't wait for an hour?"

Peter started to say something, then stopped. He glanced at Liz and Flash, and then smiled at Mary Jane, the first smile she had seen in a while. "Thanks, guys," Peter said, "for worrying. But this is going to end real soon now and then I'm going to sleep for a week, I promise." Peter held up his hand in a gesture of promise.

"We'll hold you to that. And next time you cook."

Peter laughed. "Deal." He moved quickly over and kissed Mary Jane on the cheek. "Thanks," he whispered.

"Take care," she said.

"See you guys soon," Peter said to Flash and Liz. He moved quickly toward the door and out.

After the door had closed, Mary Jane turned to her friends and shrugged. "Sorry."

"I think it actually might have helped a little," Flash said. "It always helps to know that friends are there."

"That it does," Liz said, softly.

"I think now he knows," Mary Jane said, after a moment. "You two have sure cheered me up. But I'm starving. Let's cook."

And for the next few hours Liz and Flash kept Mary Jane laughing.

# CHAPTER (7)

 Cletus Kasady wrapped the long brown winter coat closer to his body and pulled the stocking cap down over his hair. With a glance around at the crowds going and coming from cabs and shuttles, he moved into Denver International Airport's main lobby. The fresh, modern halls, shining tile, and chrome of the new airport made Kasady want to break something.

The airport was well organized and well signed. It had taken a few extra years to finish the construction and get the airport open, but in the end it had turned out perfectly, as far as most travelers were concerned. As far as Kasady thought, the place was too new and too nice to be left alone. It went against everything he believed in. Chaos should rule, not order. Denver International Airport was the king of order.

But for the moment Kasady used the order and kept silent. He had Spider-Man to take care of in New York and the easiest way to get to New York was fly. If he knew how to fly himself, he'd have stolen an airplane. But he didn't, so going by commercial plane made a lot more sense than trying to drive. Of course, after he killed Spider-Man, a drive around the country might be fun. He'd never killed anyone from Montana before.

Buying the ticket went without a problem. The man who used to own the brown coat and stocking cap Kasady now wore had kept a large stash of money in a bread box in his log cabin. Carnage had gladly relieved him of the coat, the hat, and most of the cash. He'd left five-dollar bills stuffed in the man's ears, nose, and mouth as his way of saying thank you for the coat. Actually, it had taken twenty-eight five-dollar bills in the man's mouth before he stopped breathing.

Carnage would have bet it would have taken only twenty.

With ticket in hand, Kasady made it through the underground subway and to the correct gate before trouble finally caught up with him.

The gates at Denver International were wide open lounge areas off huge, tiled halls. Four wide, moving beltways fill the center of the huge hallways, letting people ride the long distances between the gates.

It was a security guard riding one of the moving beltways who first spotted Kasady standing in a short line waiting to board a nonstop flight to LaGuardia. He obviously recognized Kasady from pictures being flashed over the police lines—or perhaps from the numerous news programs he had appeared on since he became Carnage.

Before Kasady had a chance to even hand the flight attendant his ticket three guards in blue uniforms surrounded him, their guns drawn.

"Hands up," the guard who had spotted Kasady said. He was balding with white hair, and had a stomach that rode over his belt. The other two guards were younger and very frightened. It was most likely the first time they had ever had to pull their guns outside of a training range.

Kasady looked calmly at the fat guard and smiled. "You've made what promised to be a very boring flight very interesting." In one quick movement Kasady had the flight attendant by the throat and turned around in front of him, facing the guards with the guns.

"She won't look good with holes in her," Kasady said.

"So you might want to be careful where you aim those things."

Around the boarding area a few people screamed while others scrambled to get behind seats. Then the place became unusually silent, as if the last plane of the night had landed. Even the people on the moving walkways stood silent, staring at the scene as they went past.

"Let her go," the fat guard said. "You won't get anywhere with her."

Kasady glanced at the woman. "Why not? She looks like she might be my type." He forced her head around until he was looking into her terrified eyes. "What do you think?"

The woman gave out a little squeak and that was all.

Kasady smiled at the guard. "See, she likes me."

"Let her go," the guard said.

Kasady eased his right hand across in front of the woman and scratched his left arm like he was picking at an insect bite. "I think you might want to turn and run. Around me, heroes don't seem to live very long."

As the horrified onlookers watched, Kasady changed.

A black and red flow, like blood, ran from the scratch on his arm, clinging to his legs, his arms, his head, flowing like a live animal over his skin.

Finally it covered his head, expanding and slanting his eyes into white swirling pools. His mouth grew and sprouted pointed, razor-sharp teeth. His body itself grew, seeming to suddenly dwarf the flight attendant with his mass. His skin flowed, constantly forming and changing into knives, spears, and other items of destruction on its surface.

"I warned you," Carnage said, his voice low and angry. "Little boys shouldn't play with guns." Tendrils whipped off his arm and wrapped around the three guards' guns, snapping them from their hands.

Like three extra arms, the tendrils spun the guns around a few times like old west gunfighters, then pointed the guns at the foreheads of the guards.

"Bang," Carnage said, "you're dead." The gun against the fat guard's head went off, spraying brains and blood over nearby passengers and sending the once-silent crowd running and screaming in all directions from the gate.

Carnage winked at the other two guards who stood there, faces white. "Not talking was a very smart move on your parts."

He flipped the three guns in the direction of a group of old folks, then turned the wide-eyed flight attendant around so he could look at her.

She was pretty, about twenty-five, with brown eyes and long brown hair pulled back. She wore the standard airline uniform and a wedding ring. "What's your name?" Carnage asked.

It took her a moment of swallowing before she whispered, "Louise."

"Well, Louise," Carnage said. "Since you won't go out with me, I suppose we should get on with business. Do you still need my ticket, or shall we just board?"

"Anything you want," Louise said.

Carnage let her go. "Smart woman." He bent and picked up his ticket and handed it to her. "Don't want to get in trouble with the airline, you know."

She looked shocked at the ticket in her hands, then looked up at Carnage.

"Well?" He held out his hand, waiting.

Louise glanced at his hand with the swirling skin and the needle-like nails, then at the ticket. After a moment, with her hands shaking, she managed to rip off his stub and place it in the outstretched palm of moving red and black skin.

"Thank you," Carnage said. "I assume I go this way?" He pointed down the jetway and then with a nod at Louise started in that direction, whistling.

Behind him, Louise watched him go halfway down the ramp before she fainted.

\* \* \*

Peter stood in the elevator of the *Daily Bugle* thinking about Mary Jane, Flash, and Liz as the Muzak in the background played "Happy Together." Mary Jane's attempt to cheer him up had been a nice thing to try. She was obviously worried about him and his rude reaction when they came through the door hadn't helped, he was sure.

But seeing Liz and Flash right after waking up from a dream about Gwen had been a real shock. Back when he was going out with Gwen, they had spent most of their free time with Harry, Mary Jane, and Flash. Now with sightings of Norman Osborn and the Green Goblin, he was thinking far too much about Gwen without his friends reminding him even more about her. And lately, seeing Liz served only to remind him of Harry.

He got off the elevator at the newsroom and moved across the now fairly quiet room. Only four people were in the room, all with their faces up close to computer screens. The rush to deadline was over and the next rush hadn't yet started.

An extra paper lay on a table and Peter picked it up. The headline screamed "CARNAGE ESCAPED" and below the headline was one of Peter's pictures. That would make them a little money. He always got a nice bonus when one of his photos made the front page. But he wished it wasn't for this reason.

Ben Urich was out on a story somewhere, so Peter moved over to his empty desk, glancing around to make sure no one was listening. Then he dialed Reed Richards's private line at the Fantastic Four's HQ.

Reed answered on the second ring with the words, "Reed Richards."

Peter glanced around one more time to make sure no one was listening. His spider-sense also told him the coast was clear, but it never hurt to be extra careful, especially when he was this tired. "Your friendly neighborhood wall-crawler here. Any news?"

"Nothing," Reed said. And then he hesitated. "I'm afraid we have a situation heating up outside of town. We might be gone for the next day."

"Guards still in place on the city's water supplies?"

"Yes," Reed said. "And they'll stay there until we find the serum."

"Good," Peter said. "And thanks."

There was another slight pause on the other end of the line. Then Reed said, "Did you hear Carnage escaped?"

"Afraid so," Peter said. "But really nothing on how he managed to do it."

"A large force broke in and let him out. He killed thirty or so of the people who helped him before he left on foot."

"Someone *helped* him?" Peter couldn't believe he had

even heard that. "Why would anyone do that?"

"Mercenaries, well paid and well armed," Reed said.

"But Carnage only works for himself. Everyone knows that. Why would anyone break him out?"

Another pause from Reed, then he said, "I imagine he's headed back this way, but who knows how long it might take him. You going to be all right?"

"I can always use some help with him, but I imagine it will take him some time to get here. Colorado is a ways away. So hurry back."

Reed laughed. "We will. Talk to you soon."

Reed broke the connection. Peter hung up the phone and stood staring at it for a moment. Why would anyone break Carnage out? Doing that made no sense at all.

Peter shook his head and glanced at the paper again. "Nothing these days is making any sense."

Peter dropped into Ben's chair and grabbed a scrap of paper and a pen. Time to make a list again to sort out his thinking. At the top of the paper he wrote:

*1: Dr. Catrall's serum stolen.*
*2: Pumpkin bomb used in theft.*
*3: Norman Osborn look-alike seen on street.*
*4: Green Goblin seen flying over city.*
*5: Carnage freed from the Vault by someone unknown.*

Peter sat staring at the list. The first four just might tie together. The serum was being developed from the same serum used by Norman Osborn to become the Green Goblin. But someone freeing Carnage didn't fit at all.

And what anyone would want with the serum was the biggest unanswered question.

After a moment Peter circled number five on his list. *Nothing I can do about that Carnage for the moment. But maybe I can make some headway on the first four.* Peter crumpled up the list and shoved it in his pocket, then turned and headed back for the elevator.

When he reached the second floor and the *Bugle* morgue, he smiled at Bob the computer maven. Bob, a large Irishman with silver hair and matching moustache, looked as little like a computer geek as you could imagine.

"Peter," he said, a bright smile lighting up his face. "It's been a while."

"Too long," Peter said.

"So, what vital piece of info do you need me to dig up?"

"I'm researching a possible story," Peter said. "Remember Norman Osborn?"

Bob laughed. "How could I forget him? He even came down here once with Jonah a couple months before he died. Real creepy guy as far as I was concerned."

"A lot of people thought the same thing," Peter said. Peter didn't tell him that he agreed completely. He leaned on the counter. "I was wondering if there was any way I could discover what happened to all his property? Mostly his buildings."

Bob frowned for a few moments, then moved over to the big computer on the counter. "We just might be able to. This wouldn't be possible during the day, but this time of the night I might be able to get into the city property records."

"You're not going to break in, are you?" Peter asked.

Bob laughed. "Of course not. The property records are

public record and open to everyone. It's just that during the day their computer lines are so busy I would never be able to get through.''

"Oh," Peter said. He should have known better. Bob was as straight an arrow as ever lived.

He typed like a demon for a moment on the computer terminal, then waited. After about ten seconds he said, "We're in."

His fingers went back to dancing on the keyboard. After another full minute he glanced up at Peter and then said, "Come around here and look at this."

For an instant Peter thought of just jumping over the counter, but then quickly went around to the swinging wooden gate that marked the border between morgue personnel and everyone else.

He scooted a chair over from another desk beside his and sat down.

On the computer was the name "Osborn, Norman" and a list of addresses of buildings he owned as of the year before his death.

"I figured that would be the best time to start," he said.

"Can you get a little closer to his death?" Peter asked. "Say one year later than you have there?"

"Sure," Bob said. His fingers danced on the keys and after a moment another screen full of information came up. It was a list two buildings longer than the last list.

"Boy, that guy was rich," Bob said. "Most of these addresses are downtown."

"I think his company owned more," Peter said, "but this is good enough for what I'm looking for."

"And exactly what are you looking for?" Bob asked.

Peter shrugged. "I really don't know. Just anything unusual with his property over the last month or so.''

Bob stared at him for a moment and then shook his head slowly in disbelief. ''You reporters are all alike.''

''I'm not a reporter, remember?'' Peter said. ''I'm a photographer.''

Bob laughed. ''Well, you sure are doing a good impression of a reporter tonight.''

''Thanks,'' Peter said. ''I think.''

Bob laughed again, then turned back to the computer. ''I'll just trace where each building was sold and to whom.''

He did some more fast typing and both of them sat silently staring at the screen. It became clear to Peter fairly quickly that Harry had sold off a large number of his father's buildings. And most of the rest had been sold after Harry died.

One building, across the street from the old main corporation headquarters hadn't changed hands until just recently. Then, without reason, it had a list of buyers under it that seemed to scroll on forever. All the sales had happened over a week-long period.

Peter pointed at the screen. ''Who owns that one?''

Bob studied the list for a moment. ''You know, I really can't tell. The trail on this record stops with a holding company.''

''Stops?'' Peter asked. ''Then wouldn't that holding company be the owner?''

Bob shook his head ''no.'' ''From the looks of this, part ownership of the building was sold a number of times earlier, and then split and resold. From what I understand, below a certain percentage of sale, public recording is no longer required.''

"So someone broke the ownership of this building up so many times that the true owners can no longer be traced?"

"I'd say that's what it looks like. Weird, huh?"

"Exactly what I'm looking for," Peter said. He quickly stood. "Thanks a lot." Peter headed around the counter.

"My pleasure," Bob said. "But you owe me."

Peter stopped on the other side of the counter, smiling. "And what might that be?"

"You promise you'll come back and tell me if anything comes of this. The reporters never give me the whole story that develops from what they learn here."

"I'll even bring pizza," Peter said.

"Deal," Bob shouted at his running back.

Peter entered the elevator heading to the roof. He jumped up through the trap door and changed to Spider-Man on top of the elevator.

On the roof his spider-sense told him the guys in the gray suits were still watching the roofs and probably had spotted him with night glasses.

"Don't you guys ever sleep?" Spidey said as he hit the nearest building with a web. Just before swinging out over the street he waved in the direction of the building the two men had been on earlier in the day. If they were still there and still watching, that would keep them guessing.

He swung lower between the buildings than he normally would have and by the time he reached the old Osborn-owned building on 53rd Street, just off Broadway, his spider-sense told him no one was watching.

The building was an old fifteen-story office building built back before World War II. It looked deserted and in desperate need of a facelift. Someone really had to have some money to buy this property and then let it sit like this.

Spidey found a broken out window on the second floor and crawled inside. He switched on the spider-signal on his belt—which promptly flickered and died. *Wonderful*, he thought. *A dead battery. I'm not going to find anything in here tonight, that's for sure.*

He turned and moved back to the window ledge. From the looks of the traffic it was after midnight. He might as well head for home and try to sleep again. Just the thought of sleep had him shivering.

"Get a grip, Spidey," he said to the night air. "It's just a dream. You can handle it."

He hit the neighboring building with a web and swung out over the street headed for home.

\* \* \*

Across 53rd a man in a brown coat and fedora stepped into the street and watched Spider-Man swing away.

"Didn't find anything, did you?" The man laughed. "It's time to move the plan into action."

The man moved quickly across the dark street and into a side door of the old building that Spider-Man had vacated. He went down a flight of stairs in the dark, unlocked a door, and went inside.

A dusty, empty, windowless basement room was all the one light showed. The man paid no attention. He moved quickly to a blank wall and pushed slightly. The wall slid back without a sound. Beyond was a plush office, with bookcases and a huge desk.

The man moved to the desk and picked up the container

that held Dr. Catrall's serum. He opened it and stared at the glistening liquid inside.

Soon revenge would be his. Spider-Man would be driven over the edge into insanity.

The man laughed as he carefully replaced the vial. "An insane Spider-Man. Oh, won't this be fun to watch?"

# CHAPTER (8)

Carnage ambled down the jetway and onto the plane. Two of the flight attendants saw him first. One screamed and ran for the back of the plane. The other stood in the food preparation area, her hand over her mouth, her eyes wide with fear.

Carnage nodded at her. "I hope we have a smooth flight, don't you?"

Her eyes grew even wider and slowly she nodded.

Carnage smiled at her. Then he turned toward the front and in a dozen quick strides through first class was in the cockpit area.

All three of the flight crew were in their places, headphones on. The two men and one woman turned and stared as Carnage slammed open the cockpit door and bent to enter.

Carnage glanced at all the instruments and the three crew. "I have a very important date in New York. Can we get this flight started?"

The pilot, a solid, gray-haired man in his early fifties shook his head "no." "The tower's not giving us clearance."

"Then you'll just have to take off without it, won't you?"

"I can't," he said, raising his hands in a gesture of helplessness. "They have the wheels blocked down below and we have to be pushed back from the gate."

Carnage nodded. "I should be able to take care of that. Be ready to go." He turned and moved back into the plane. The aisles were crowded with panicked people all rushing to get out the one door.

"Everyone sit down!" Carnage shouted.

He waited a moment and then walked toward the door, brushing people aside like so much dust. Bodies tumbled over seats and smashed into one another. One man in a gray sweater couldn't get out of the way quickly enough. Carnage picked him up by the head and yanked.

Blood spurted everywhere. Carnage held the head up and looked at the bloody, shocked face as the man's headless body fell into a sitting position in a seat.

Around the body, people were choking and throwing up, most of them unable to look away.

"This should do just fine," Carnage said.

Carrying the head by the hair like it was a suitcase, he moved to the entrance of the plane and walked a few feet up the jetway to the corner. There he could see the police at the top where he'd given the attendant his ticket.

The last of the passengers to get out were just clearing the door at the top. Carnage waited until only the police were visible, then shouted, "If this jet is not pushed back in five minutes, I will bring you another one of these."

Like a bowling ball, he hurled the head up the jetway. It rolled like a football, bumping and spinning in odd ways until it smashed with a sickening thump into the wall near the door at the top. "Strike," Carnage said, laughing. "I forgot how much fun bowling can be."

Still laughing, he moved back into the plane. "Close that door now," he said to the flight attendant close by. He stood and watched while she did what she was told.

"Prepare for takeoff," Carnage said. "I would imagine we will be leaving soon."

The flight attendant nodded. Without so much as a glance around at the cowering people he moved toward the cockpit. He stuck his head in the door. "Captain, I think I have gotten us clearance."

The captain nodded, his face very white.

"Would you please be so kind as to tell the tower to relay a message to New York for me?"

Again all the captain could do was nod "yes."

"Have them tell Spider-Man that I am coming."

Carnage turned and went back into first class.

He stood staring out over the seats and the people. "Everyone back into the cattle car."

It took a moment, but then the people moved quickly, scrambling toward the back of the plane. After they were all gone he dropped down into an empty seat in the first row. He turned and motioned for the flight attendant to come forward. When she was standing in the aisle beside him he turned and asked, "Do you know if they're showing a movie on this flight?"

*  *  *

For the first time in two weeks Peter managed to get three hours of restless sleep before the nightmare drove him from the warm bed and Mary Jane's side.

Outside it was still pitch black and probably cold. The apartment sure felt cold. He glanced at the clock. With winter coming, the sunrise wouldn't be for another two hours. The early morning staff at the *Daily Bugle* would be going at full speed about now. He might as well head down there and see what Carnage was up to. And get his mind off the dreams and the lack of sleep.

As he got up Mary Jane looked up at him. "You all right?"

"Just more dreams," Peter said. "But I did get some sleep this time. And I feel a little better."

"Good," Mary Jane said, snuggling back down into the blankets. "Come back to bed soon."

Peter looked at his beautiful wife snuggled under the warm quilts and then at the dark outside. It was tempting to crawl back in beside her. But then the image of Gwen falling from the bridge and the Green Goblin laughing as she fell into a mouth of blood made him stand and head for his clothes. He got three hours of sleep, there was no point in tempting fate. For the first time in weeks he felt like he had a little energy.

Fifteen minutes later, after a small breakfast of cold cereal, he was swinging toward the *Bugle*. As he neared the main area of town his spider-sense buzzed—he was being watched. Two of the guys in gray suits stood on a nearby building, tracking him like he was an enemy craft.

"This is getting annoying, guys," Spider-Man said. He dropped toward the street below, swinging low over the traffic. But somehow his spider-sense told him they were still managing to track him, even in the dark.

"See if you can follow me underground," he said aloud in the direction of two gray-suited men on a nearby roof. He swung down and dropped into a subway staircase.

"Spider-Man! Wow!"

Peter glanced around. Three high-school-aged boys had been coming up the stairs when he had appeared in front of them. All three had long raincoats and the tallest wore a black, wide-brimmed hat. They had stopped just below where he clung to the wall.

"You guys are sure up early."

The tallest shrugged. "School field trip. Had to catch the subway in."

"You want to do a fella a favor? Won't take long."

"Anything for you," the tallest said, coming up a few steps farther.

Spidey dropped to the stairs. His spider-sense had calmed. No one was watching him from above and the kids were of no danger to him.

"I need to meet someone at the *Daily Bugle*, but I got these guys watching me from the tops of the buildings. Could I borrow your coat and hat and walk with you guys the block to the *Bugle* building?"

Before Spidey was even finished talking the tall kid had his coat off and was handing it over.

"Cool," one of the others said. "Helping Spider-Man."

Spidey slipped the coat over his costume and put on the offered hat, snuggling it down low on his forehead. "How do I look?"

The tall kid laughed. "Like Spider-Man wearing a coat and hat."

"Thanks," Spidey said, laughing with him. "But in the dark it just might work. Shall we give it a try?"

The three boys surrounded him and as a unit they all climbed the stairs, turning to the right at the top.

His spider-sense stayed quiet as the four of them strolled toward the *Daily Bugle* building. "So far so good."

"Man, how can you tell?" one of the boys asked.

"I just sort of *know*."

"Cool," the youngest boy said, his voice full of awe.

They made it through the front door of the *Bugle* without problems and only a few stares from passersby. Spidey peeled off the coat and hat and handed it back to the tall kid. "Thanks, I owe you one."

The tall kid shook his head "no." "You saved my mom about a year ago from some muggers." He slipped his coat back on. "I think I still owe you a few."

Spider-Man stared at the kid for a moment as he finished putting on his hat. Sometimes, in all the problems, Spidey forgot that what he did affected real people, people with lives and families. He couldn't remember who the kid's mom was. Probably he actually hadn't met her, just stopped the mugging and went on into the night. But his actions helped people and that was why he did what he did. He had been given the power and using it right was his responsibility. He'd learned that the night Uncle Ben died.

But with fighting Carnage and searching for a vial full of deadly serum, he sometimes forgot he did it all to help others. Today, here in the lobby of the *Daily Bugle*, with people staring from all sides, he had been reminded.

"What's your name?" Spider-Man asked.

The kid looked at Spider-Man for a moment, then said, "Alan. Alan Conners."

"Alan Conners, I think you just paid me back more than you might ever know. Thanks."

Without looking back, he bounded quickly up the wide staircase, jumping over people as he went. On the mezzanine level he found the door to the fire stairs and went inside. Three stories up his spider-sense told him the coast was clear.

Quickly he changed into his regular clothes, and a few minutes later Peter Parker opened the door into the newsroom. For some reason the room seemed even noisier and more hectic than usual. Everyone seemed to be running at top speed on some errand or another.

"Peter!" The voice of *Bugle* City Editor Kathryn Cushing caught him before he got two steps into the room.

Kate stood in her office door, her arm waving. Peter held up his hand indicating he was on his way, then quickly threaded his way through the busy room. A copy of the morning edition of the *Bugle* laying on one desk caught his attention and he stopped. His stomach clamped around the breakfast he'd just eaten. The headline read: "CARNAGE TO SPIDER-MAN: 'I'M ON MY WAY'."

Peter scanned the rest of the article. It seemed that late last night Carnage had hijacked a jetliner at Denver International. The plane was due into LaGuardia at six a.m.

Peter glanced up at the wall clock. Quarter after five. He had forty-five minutes to get to the airport. He could make it.

"Peter!" Kate's voice again cut through the bedlam of the newsroom.

Peter turned around to see the blonde woman storming in his direction, reporters and staff moving deftly out of her way.

Kate pointed at the paper Peter was holding. "You're up to speed on what happened, so get a camera and get out to the airport. I want pictures and lots of them."

"On my way," Peter said, but Kate had already walked off to talk to someone else. Kate Cushing was not one to mess around when big news was breaking.

Peter turned and ran toward the main door of the room, running the maze between the desks like a running back. He hoped his automatic camera would get some good shots so he could make a little extra money. But if he didn't, it didn't matter. Carnage was all that mattered.

Less than twenty seconds later he was opening the door to the roof when his spider-sense warned him of trouble. Normally he changed clothes between some air-conditioning ducts on the roof, but this morning he didn't have that option. The guys in the gray suits were out there watching. At this time of day, the top-of-the-elevator trick would not work.

The sun was just coming up through high clouds, sending orange and red streaks over the city. Peter held the door open just an inch, staring out. Two men in gray suits, ties neatly in place, stood on the top of the building across the street. One wore the weird-looking pilot's helmet. They had a clear view of the top of the *Daily Bugle*.

"Do you guys ever take a break?" he said out loud. His voice echoed in the metal stairwell.

Peter let the door close and his spider-sense dimmed to almost nothing. "Might as well change right here."

As quickly as he could he had on his Spider-Man costume and his camera in its usual spot on his belt.

He hit the door at a run, banging it open. He was off the side of the building and swinging through the air over the street before the gray-suited goons even had a chance to turn around.

But his spider-sense was going wild. They were watching him from two or three directions, of that there was no doubt.

He hit the next building over with another web and swung to the top of a shorter office building. He started across the corner of the building roof when his spider-sense went totally wild. There didn't seem to be any place to escape to.

He jumped, hoping against hope it was the right move to make.

It wasn't.

A high-pitched sound filled his head and the world around him seemed to go totally nuts.

Everything blurred. Blue-green lights flashed behind his eyes. The world was spinning like a carnival ride out of control and Spidey just wished for a way off.

He made two staggering steps toward the edge of the building and then went to his knees. Through the spinning, flashing lights he saw two men in gray suits on the building across the street. One was wearing a helmet and the other was pointing a rifle-like thing at him.

The city spun around him for what seemed like an eternity, mixing with the blue and orange colors of the beautiful morning sky.

Then everything went black.

* * *

The dark basement office in the old Osborn building was still mostly covered in dust. The desk had been cleaned and a new computer installed on it. But the books that filled the bookcases hadn't been touched. A hidden door stood open, leading to the large warehouse space beyond.

On a workbench near the door were two goblin-gliders and a number of pumpkin bombs. Other bombs hung on the wall along with a half dozen pairs of sparkle gloves.

The man from Chicago, wearing a white lab coat and rubber gloves, stood over the table. Dr. Catrall's vial of serum was in front of him beside an open pumpkin bomb.

Slowing, acting as if the serum might explode at any moment, the man carefully took an eyedropper of the liquid and dropped one drop at a time into the open top of one pumpkin bomb. Six drops total. Then he carefully closed the lid of the vial and after that the top of the pumpkin bomb.

He held the pumpkin bomb up, turning it one way, than the other. *Spider-Man*, he thought, *when you show up at the airport to meet Carnage, you'll be in for a surprise.*

The man sat the bomb down on the counter near one glider. *In fact, you'll lose your mind over this surprise.*

The man's laughter echoed through the empty warehouse space and died in the dark corners and cobwebs.

*That's done.* He stood back and stared at the bomb, then clapped his hands together and took off the rubber gloves. *Time to get all of Gwen Stacy's old friends together for a little reunion. A very short-lived one.*

Again he laughed as he moved into the office and behind the desk. He dropped into the high-backed chair facing a computer screen. He had learned from the Goblin's records he had found at Kraven the Hunter's home that Spider-Man had almost gone insane when Gwen Stacy died. So it seemed logical that Spider-Man might also have some feelings for her other close friends.

The screen showed files for Flash Thompson, Peter Parker, Mary Jane Watson-Parker, and Harry Osborn's widow, Liz.

"You four should do just fine." He reached for the phone and started dialing.

# CHAPTER (9)

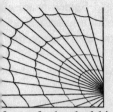 Spider-Man slowly came back to consciousness as four men in gray suits gathered around him. He kept very still, letting the spinning in his head clear. The cool morning air was quickly clearing away the effects of what had hit him. If he just lay still and played dead, he might almost be back to full strength before they knew what was going on.

"Did you kill him?" one guy with a high voice asked.

"These things couldn't kill anyone," another man answered. "They just make people dizzy and pass out. Besides, he's still breathing."

"And you sprayed that entire building over there when you hit him," another voice said. "Bogal isn't going to be happy about that."

"I got Spider-Man, didn't I? That's all Bogal's going to care about. And all I care about is the bonus for catching him."

"Bonus, hah!"

Another man grunted in agreement. "You'll be lucky if Bogal doesn't kill you right out."

From the sound of the voices and the footsteps on the roof, Spider-Man could tell that the men had him completely surrounded.

But why and who did they work for? Bogal, whoever he was, seemed to be the goon in charge. That might be a good piece of information to know.

The spinning behind Spidey's eyes was slowing. He took a very slow, very deep breath while keeping his eyes closed, and the last of the spinning cleared.

Across the roof a door opened, and Spidey heard all four men turn to look. A perfect time for a surprise attack.

He was on his feet before any of the men even realized he'd moved.

Four quick punches and the men were down and out cold.

The guy coming from the door wasn't armed. He stopped with a very surprised look on his face.

"That was almost too easy," Spidey said out loud, then realized he might have spoken just a little too soon. His spider-sense was going off like a four-alarm fire bell in his head.

Two men in gray suits stood on a nearby building. One of them had a funny-looking rifle aimed at him. They were going to spray their own men to capture him, as well as anyone inside this building and the building beyond.

Spidey dove over the edge and into a full free fall for the street, letting gravity speed him away.

*Those guys are no FBI*, Spidey thought as he dropped down the side of the building. FBI men were crazy at times, but they weren't totally nuts. And the FBI usually didn't go around shooting entire buildings full of people.

As he fell, his spider-sense went wild, telling him there was no place to go for safety. The beam caught him halfway down the building, sending the world around him spinning like a child's top.

He was falling toward the street. The effects of the ray might only knock him out, but a fall from this height would kill him. He had to do something and do it quick.

With everything going black and white and spinning like a drunk's bedroom, he managed to shoot a web out in the direction he guessed was a building. The web caught on the edge of a window and swung him hard against the side of the building, knocking the wind out of him. But the impact cleared his head for a fraction of a second.

He dropped the last two stories to the sidewalk and staggered down into a subway staircase. It was still early and a train had just pulled out, so the station was mostly empty. He staggered past a few arriving commuters and down onto the lowest platform. Only one woman stood there reading a paper and waiting.

With the tunnel spinning and blue and white flashes clouding his vision, he dropped down onto the track and staggered up into the welcome darkness of the tunnel.

The only thought going through his mind was that he had to find a safe place.

A place safe from the men in the gray suits, safe from Carnage, safe from whoever had the serum.

Safe from nightmares.

Fifteen feet up the track was a small, box-sized hole in the side of the old brick wall. He dropped to the dirt and crawled into the hole.

The hole was filled with spider webs and felt damp under his hands.

Perfect.

He let himself collapse to the floor of the hole. His dizziness made the single spider seem like a thousand spiders surrounding him, covering him in a thousand strands of web, protecting him.

"Just a short nap, friend," Spidey said to the spider.

As a train thundered past just outside the hole in the brick, Spider-Man passed out.

* * *

K.L. Bogal stood facing the five men on the rooftop. They were standing at attention in a very straight line, waiting as he paced back and forth. Bogal had gotten a call ten minutes earlier that Spider-Man had been captured. Then on the way here he heard his men scrambling, shouting in their headphones that Spider-Man had gotten away. Now, beside being angry, he needed to know exactly what happened.

He stopped and faced the men. "Go over this very slowly and carefully. You had him, is that right? Williams?"

The man on the far left very quietly said, "Yes sir."

"And he was knocked out?"

"Yes, sir," Williams said again.

"By who and from what building?"

Williams pointed to the south. "Kelly got him, sir, using a wide beam."

"A wide beam?" Bogal shook his head in disbelief. Bogal look in the direction Williams had pointed. Across the street was a block-wide office building that had also been sprayed by Kelly. It was lucky it was early or there would have been thousands of sick and injured in that building. He had no doubt there were enough early workers in there who had become dizzy and fainted to cause the police and health officials to investigate.

Bogal turned and stared at Kelly for a moment, then went back to speaking to Williams. "Then what happened?"

"Spider-Man suddenly sprang to his feet and knocked

the four of us out cold. He was incredibly fast. Faster than anything I've ever seen move.''

"That's because he's a super hero, you idiot,'' Bogal said. "So no one stood away from him and kept him covered as you were trained to do?''

"He was out cold,'' Williams said softly.

Bogal stared at him for a moment, then shook his head in total disgust. He hadn't expected these men to be brain surgeons, but he had expected them to at least follow their training.

Bogal sighed. "So what happened next?''

Williams pointed to the north edge of the building. "Spider-Man dove over there and Brady on the building across the street there got a shot at him.''

"While he was falling!'' Bogal shouted. Spider-Man could have been killed and then he would have been no use at all for getting the serum back. His men were all total idiots. He would personally make sure Brady paid for such stupidity.

"I don't know, sir,'' Williams said. "I was out cold at that moment.''

Bogal shook his head side to side. "So what happened to Spider-Man?''

Williams shrugged. "No one saw. He shot a web at a building and swung out of sight below. He disappeared down on the street somewhere.''

"At least you idiots didn't kill him.'' Bogal let out a sigh of relief and moved over to the edge of the building.

Below, the morning commute was starting to fill the sidewalks and the streets. Yellow cabs ebbed and flowed like blood in a vein. Construction hammering had started somewhere in the direction of uptown, echoing through the canyons between the buildings like distant gunshots in the mountains during hunting season.

A typical morning in New York.

"Where did you go, Spider-Man?" Bogal said to the streets below, his voice lost in the normal sounds. Spider-Man was now on notice of what Bogal and his weapons could do. Bogal knew the wall-crawler wouldn't be such an easy catch next time.

Bogal turned and faced his men. "Inform everyone to return to headquarters at once. Wait there on two-minute readiness for my call."

"Yes, sir," Williams said.

Bogal turned back to look out over the city. At least with Spider-Man knowing he was after him, it would be a fair fight. Bogal liked it much better that way.

Below and around the neighboring blocks, police and ambulance sirens were blaring, pulling up at the buildings partially full of the sick, innocent victims from the attack against Spider-Man.

Bogal didn't even notice.

Or for that matter, much care.

# CHAPTER 10

The early morning hadn't really gone as Mary Jane had planned. First, Peter got up and left way before sunrise. And then Flash Thompson had awoken her a half hour before her alarm. Liz Osborn had arrived less than a minute later and now her two guests were sitting with her at the kitchen table, drinking coffee and talking.

Mary Jane had managed to slip into the bedroom and pull on some jeans and a sweatshirt, but that was as much as she'd managed. Her teeth needed brushing, her hair needed washing and she felt just all around grungy. Certainly not the way she would have liked to entertain guests, even old friends.

The three of them had been trying to figure out who had called Flash and Liz and told them to meet at Mary Jane's and Peter's apartment. No one had called Mary Jane and told her. She had an audition in two hours and she didn't want to miss it.

"His voice was deep and full, almost like a radio jock's," Flash said.

Liz nodded in agreement. "A trained voice all right. No doubt about that. He said it was important. That he had information about Harry's father and about how he died."

"Really?" Flash asked. "The guy told me it was information about Gwen."

A very thick silence filled the room. Finally Mary Jane couldn't stand the thought of how Gwen died any longer. "Weird," Mary Jane said, sipping on her coffee. "Very weird.'' She felt a shiver run up her spine and she took another sip of coffee to calm it and to help clear her head.

A loud knock on the front door startled all three of them.

''Careful,'' Flash said and Mary Jane nodded.

All three of them went to the front door, but Flash stood off to one side and slightly behind the front door, just in case he needed to jump whoever came through the door.

''Who is it?'' Mary Jane said after trying to see through the peephole in the door. She could see that someone was there, and that it was a man, but he was a blur.

Then in an instant her mind realized why. He was coming at the door hard. It was only instinct that got her head and face away from the wood in time. A loud crash sent the door smashing inward. Wood splinters scattered over the room like confetti.

Mary Jane took most of the force of the door against her shoulder and it sent her flying backwards into Liz. Both of them ended up in a pile on the couch, Mary Jane mostly on top.

''Don't,'' a deep voice said with authority.

Mary Jane managed to scramble up first. She could tell her shoulder was going to be sore for weeks, but otherwise she was okay.

A medium-sized man with close-cut and receding red-brown hair stood facing Flash with a gun. Flash slowly raised his hands in the air as the man kicked what was left of the door closed behind him.

Mary Jane turned and helped Liz up. ''You all right?'' Liz nodded and then they both turned toward the man.

''All right,'' Mary Jane started to say. ''What do—''

Beside her, Mary Jane heard Liz gasp. But there was

no need to ask why. She could see the man just fine and he looked very, very familiar.

Mary Jane, her mouth still open in the middle of her question glanced at Flash, who also looked shocked.

The man turned slightly to face Liz, the gun moving with him to end up pointing at her chest. ''What's the matter,'' he asked, a smile on his face. ''Don't you recognize your father-in-law?''

\* \* \*

The smell of damp earth and mold made Spider-Man cough.

He opened his eyes to the dark of a small, confined area. He was curled up on his side on damp ground, facing a wall. A faint light from over his shoulder lit up an old brick wall and the ground in front of his face. Both spun slowly along with small blue stars behind his eyelids and around his vision.

The small spider had crawled into the corner above him and seemed to be waiting for him to leave. He stared at the spider for a moment. ''Thanks for the use of your home,'' he said to the spider. ''But I think it's time for me to move along.''

He pushed himself up slowly, his head bumping slightly against the ceiling of the small hole. Then, his head still spinning he started to push himself backwards out of the hole. *Funny*, he thought, *last time I was in these tunnels, I took a nap, too.* Back then, he was chasing an alien creature that had taken up residence in these tunnels. *It wasn't any more pleasant then either*, he decided.

His spider-sense went off like a too-loud alarm, so he stopped. *Those gray-suited goons can't be down here, too.*

He twisted around, but by the time he had his head into position to look down the tunnel he understood what the problem was. The ground was shaking and it wasn't an aftereffect of getting shot with that weird rifle. No, there was a large light headed his way through the tunnel.

He pulled his head back into the hole and waited. Slowly the rumbling in the ground grew into a huge sound that seemed to vibrate every shaky nerve and brain cell Spidey had. Flashing lights and screeching of wheels on rails filled the small hole like a punk band gone bad.

Then, faster than it had taken to build, it was past.

*Hope that was the only one*, Spidey thought, shaking his head to clear his ears as he pushed himself out of his hiding place. He stood and, leaning against the wall, watched the train as it sped through the lights of the distant station without stopping.

*Express. Might have guessed.*

He continued to lean against the wall, waiting for his head to stop spinning. The effects were clearing quickly. After a moment he pushed off from the brick and walked slowly toward the station.

By the time he had made it back to the station platform and the bright light he was feeling better, and the world seemed to be slowing its spin.

He just hoped he wasn't too late to meet Carnage's plane.

* * *

But Spider-Man was too late. As he was crawling out of the hole in the subway tunnel, Carnage's plane touched down.

The DC-10 taxied to a slow stop at the end of a runway

where it was instantly surrounded by two hundred cops and military police, all pointing guns at the plane. A police helicopter circled overhead and in the distance three press helicopters flew small circling patterns.

Held back a safe distance behind police lines were another few thousand onlookers and reporters. They were all there to witness firsthand the rematch between Carnage and Spider-Man. National television cameras were set up on trucks along the lines. Around the world, stations broke from regular programming to cut live to the scene. The entire world had witnessed the last fight between Spider-Man and Carnage and they were all interested in the rematch.

After a few minutes of the plane simply sitting quietly at the end of the runway, a buzz started through the thousands of onlookers outside the police lines.

''Where's Spider-Man?''

''Maybe he isn't going to show up.''

''Maybe he's afraid.''

Inside the plane, Carnage sat waiting.

# CHAPTER 11

 Spider-Man got a few odd stares from waiting subway travelers as he jumped up on the platform. He ignored them and bounded up the stairs, almost without getting dizzy. But his spider-sense warned him before he reached the top. There was danger on the sidewalk.

"Give me a break," he muttered. He was getting really annoyed at these gray-suited guys. He climbed up on the ceiling of the staircase, trying to get a glance at who or what was causing his spider-sense to go nuts.

The sidewalks were starting to fill with workers as the time neared seven a.m. The gray-suited goons seemed to be everywhere. It was like a plague of them, coming out of the buildings up and down the street as far as Spidey could see.

*Who* are *these guys? And why do they want me?*

He hung from the ceiling and stared out at the street. If he made a rush at the side of the nearest building he'd be picked off with the strange ray gun before he could reach the top.

If he went right at some of them, he'd never get to them all before being zapped into a spinning black hell. And after being hit with that stupid thing twice, he had no intention of ever having it happen again.

He slammed his fist into the ceiling, punching a small dent in the old concrete. He was sorely tempted to walk right out on the street and yell "Go home!" at the gray-suited idiots.

He slammed his fist into the concrete again and a fine

dust and a small chunk of rock rained down on the stairs.

*Get a grip on yourself, Spidey. You're tired. Losing it here won't help.*

But he had to be at the airport when Carnage's plane landed. Time was running out, if it wasn't already too late. There was no telling how many lives would be lost if he didn't meet that plane. He couldn't let a bunch of yuppies with toy guns stop him.

Below him, a train rumbled to a stop at the subway station.

Spidey stared at the gray suits on the sidewalk, then dropped to the stairs and ran for the train.

He caught the subway door of the last car as it was closing and squeezed inside.

A young teenage couple sat holding hands near the front of the car and an elderly woman clutched a brown purse in a center seat. Otherwise the car was empty.

Spidey took a hold of a bar as the train lurched into motion and looked down at the woman. ''Sometimes commuting to work is sure tough.''

The woman clutched her purse even tighter to her chest, stood, and scampered toward the door leading into the forward cars. As she left both teenagers laughed and gave Spidey a thumbs up.

After dealing with all the yuppies in gray suits, it was nice to have fans.

\* \* \*

Flash Thompson twisted at the ropes that held his wrists. He could feel the thin, rough texture of the rope cutting into his skin, but he ignored the pain. Getting out of here was much more important. He glanced around Mary Jane

142

and Peter's apartment for anything he might be able to use to get himself free.

Nothing.

Beside him on the couch, Mary Jane and Liz fought against their ropes. They didn't look as if they were having any better luck than he was.

"How long has he been gone?" Liz whispered.

"Maybe a minute," Mary Jane said, also whispering. "Do you think maybe it's time we do some screaming for help?"

The man who looked and talked exactly like the late Norman Osborn had tied them up hands and feet, deposited them on the couch like so many stuffed dolls, and then just left. No reason, no instructions, nothing.

"I think it's time," Flash said. He could feel the ropes on his hands starting to loosen just a little. He went at them even harder, twisting and working to find any way to slip out. He could feel the sharp biting pain of his skin being rubbed off, but he ignored it and kept twisting.

Almost simultaneously, both Mary Jane and Liz, in their highest, sharpest, and most penetrating voices screamed, "Help!" Flash couldn't imagine why they wouldn't be heard clear down in midtown.

From that point on they alternated yelling for a good minute. But as hard as Flash listened he couldn't hear anyone pounding up the stairs to their rescue.

No footsteps running in the hall. Nothing.

"Don't you have neighbors?" Flash asked between calls for help. He just couldn't believe there weren't ten people outside the door as loud as they were shouting.

"Probably all on their way to work or school by now," Mary Jane said.

Mary Jane was just taking a deep breath for another call for help when the window exploded inward, showering the room in glass.

Flash ducked, protecting his eyes from the glass. Two pieces bounced off his back and his lap was covered.

The Green Goblin, laughing like crazy, circled the room on his jet glider, knocking over a lamp.

He did another quick circle, then landed the glider in front of them. Flash couldn't believe his eyes. First Norman Osborn and now the Green Goblin. This was just too strange. And what did the Goblin want with them?

Like she weighed nothing at all, the Goblin picked up Mary Jane and flipped her over his shoulder. She did her best to kick and fight back, but with her hands tied, it was useless.

Flash struggled even harder with his bonds, fighting to get free to help her.

No luck at all. He was tied tight.

The Goblin got back on his glider and with a high, insane laugh, took off out the window, banging Mary Jane's leg on the edge of the window as he went.

"We've got to get out of here, now!" Flash said. "Twist around here and let me see if I can loosen your ropes with my fingers."

Liz did as he told her, and Flash turned his back on her and moved in close. He could feel the ropes holding her hands with his numb fingers. Blood dripped down onto her wrist and into her palm, making them slick. The knots felt tight, very tight.

"You have any feeling in your fingers?" Flash asked her.

"Some," Liz said.

"My ropes are looser than yours. See what you can do."

Flash moved his bonds into her hands and he could feel her frantically working at the knot. Suddenly something seemed to loosen.

"Wait," he said. Using all his strength in his shoulders, he twisted and turned, pulling one hand free. "Got it!"

Quickly, he twisted around and untied Liz's hands. Then they both went to work on their leg bonds and a moment later were standing.

"Where to?" Liz asked, rubbing her wrists. Flash could see that her face was white and she was about to panic.

"Out the door and hide," Flash said, heading for the door. "And fast."

Flash yanked the door open for Liz, then closed it behind them. Two doors down the hall there was a door labeled "Utilities."

Liz went by it, heading for the stairs. "Liz. In here."

The door was locked, but Flash had so much adrenaline pumping in his blood that he yanked on the door and the old lock broke. Inside were brooms, a bucket and mop, and a small sink.

Flash pulled the door closed just as a crash came from Mary Jane's apartment.

A moment later they could hear swearing.

The door to the apartment opened, then a moment later slammed shut. More cursing and another crash of something falling.

Then all was silent.

Flash finally let out the breath he'd been holding for as long as he could remember.

Beside him he heard Liz do the same.

After a few long moments while Flash strained to hear

any sound at all, Liz whispered, "Did he leave?"

"I don't know," Flash whispered back. "But I think we should stay right here for a while to make sure."

"No argument from me."

She put her arms around his waist and hugged him.

Twenty minutes later they finally sneaked out of the closet and down the stairs to the street.

By the time they found a cop everyone in the city and around the world knew what was going on.

\* \* \*

On top of one of the main stone support pillars of the Brooklyn Bridge, Mary Jane lay flat, her hands and feet tied. The cold wind off the river had numbed her skin and she was afraid to even roll over for fear of falling off. This was the same bridge, the same pillar where the Green Goblin had killed Gwen Stacy.

Now she was here.

Her worst nightmare had come true.

And Peter's.

The Goblin had left her, promising to return. The moment he was back over the city she started yelling for help. Intellectually, she knew this was pointless. No one was likely to be able to hear her. Even if someone did hear, she had no idea what they could do about it.

But she had to do *something*. And maybe somebody would hear.

\* \* \*

The DC-10 carrying Carnage and eighty-six passengers sat at the end of the runway. Even though it was surrounded by hundreds of men with guns and thousands and thousands of gawkers, the plane looked naked and alone. The early morning sun did little to take the feeling of doom off the picture.

Nothing had moved from the plane for twenty minutes. Not since it rolled to a stop. The pilots had not even communicated with the tower and could not be seen in the cockpit windows.

At twenty minutes and seventeen seconds from the moment the plane touched down, the door closest to the front opened.

The television cameras mounted on the trucks sent the picture of that plane and that door to millions of sets in homes and offices around the world. It seemed like collectively, everyone in the world held their breath.

And waited.

Two terrified women, one a flight attendant, the other a blond passenger, suddenly filled the doorway. Red and black tendrils were wrapped around them, moving constantly like a lover's hands.

The two women were thrust out into the open air and Carnage filled the door. He held the women over the long drop to the pavement. Both women kicked and fought, but the tendrils that held them in the air didn't even seem to notice their weight or their fight.

Carnage surveyed the scene around the plane, the spectators and press beyond the distant fence. Then in a voice loud enough, it seemed, to carry halfway into the city, he shouted, "Where's Spider-Man?"

The words echoed off the runway. No one around the plane moved.

Disgusted, Carnage lifted the blond passenger high into the air. She wore long black slacks and a white jacket.

Her legs pumped the air like she was running hard. Like she was nothing more than a baseball, Carnage tossed her overhand in the direction of the press trucks.

Thousands screamed with the woman as she flailed her arms, seemingly trying to fly.

Millions more around the world gasped in horror as the cameramen did their job and followed the high arc of the woman's flight above the runway.

Her body hit the dirt beside the runway and bounced once like a rag doll, rolling a few times before it came to a stop.

The telephoto cameras on the distant trucks showed blood running from her mouth into the dirt. The look on her face was frozen in pure terror.

"I want Spider-Man!" Carnage's voice shouted over the stunned crowd.

He held the flight attendant up high for a moment. "Until Spider-Man shows up here, I will kill one person every five minutes. Understand?"

He stared around at the police, then pulled the flight attendant back inside the plane.

The door closed.

# CHAPTER 12

 The cold wind chilled Mary Jane to the bone and her voice was going raw from shouting. She knew her wrists were bleeding from struggling with the rope because she could feel the warm blood.

She was laying on her side on the bird dropping-covered stone, facing the city across the river. She desperately wanted to sit up to see if anyone was coming to her rescue, but she didn't dare. The wind was just a little too strong and if she lost her balance and rolled the wrong way, she'd die.

"Oh, no," she said softly. From the general direction of her Upper East Side apartment she could see the Green Goblin returning on his glider, soaring out over the water. There was no one with him. She fought down the fear that he had killed Flash and Liz.

*Maybe they got away*, she thought firmly, forcing the thought of their deaths out of her mind. *They got away. I'm sure of it. They must have.*

She couldn't believe all this was happening. First Norman Osborn tied them up at gunpoint and then the Green Goblin took her out the window. Was Norman Osborn really alive?

Could that be possible?

If so, Peter was in real trouble. He had always felt that it was his fault that Gwen died. And with the Goblin back, he would be tortured by guilt even more.

The Goblin circled the pillar and then landed beside her, right in front of her face so that she could see him from where she lay.

"Your friends managed to get away," he said. "And I never did find that husband of yours."

She could tell he wasn't happy with that, so she said nothing, even though her heart was racing and she wanted to cheer. No point in making him angry, considering that all it would take would be a nudge from him and she'd die in the cold water hundreds of feet below.

He looked out over the city and then down at the river. Suddenly the Goblin brightened and let out with a long, cackling laugh that seemed to cut into her very heart.

He leaned in closer to her, tipping his head so he could look her directly in the eye. "You know, actually, this might even be better. Gwen Stacy was the only one up here the first time. It will drive Spider-Man even crazier to have the same thing happen to you, don't you think?"

He looked down at Mary Jane with those evil eyes and laughed in her face. "I asked you a question."

Mary Jane stayed perfectly still and after a moment he straightened up and turned away. "Just don't know what I was thinking, wanting all four of you up here." His laugh carried out over the water. "That would have been too crowded."

Mary Jane again didn't say a word or move a muscle, even though the insane laugh made her want to shout in agony. This felt like a nightmare, a dream she would wake up from at any moment, but from the numbing cold she knew it wasn't.

After a moment, the Goblin mounted his glider again. "Now don't go rolling around. I've got a fight to check on and a Spider-Man to drive crazy." That got him laughing long and hard.

Mary Jane shuddered and lay still as the Goblin circled

once over her on his glider and sped away. "Peter, where are you?" she whispered.

* * *

The Goblin was shocked with what he found at the airport.

The DC-10 airliner sat alone at the end of a runway, surrounded by what seemed like hundreds of armed troops and thousands of spectators and press. But there was no fight going on at all.

No sign of Spider-Man. No sign of Carnage.

Staying high and out of range of the rifles below, the Goblin circled for a moment above the helicopter, then dove the glider in fast until he was hovering just outside the door to the plane.

In that position, the police wouldn't dare fire at him for fear of hitting someone in the plane. But just in case, he kept moving back and forth.

"Carnage!" Goblin shouted. "You in there?"

After a moment the door hissed open and Carnage stepped forward holding a terrified flight attendant over the long drop to the pavement.

"I see you've been enjoying your flight," Goblin said.

Carnage looked at him for a moment, then said, "I thought you were dead."

The Goblin, who had stopped moving and now hovered on his glider across the open air from Carnage, laughed. "Does it matter?"

Carnage shook his head sending drips of black and red flying in all directions. "Not to me." He stared at the Goblin for a moment, then asked, "You're the one who arranged, or should I say, *paid* for my release?"

"From what I saw on the news, a lot of Vault Guardsmen and my men paid for your release with their lives."

Carnage laughed this time. "Does it matter?"

"Not to me," Goblin said. Together they both laughed.

"I have a proposition for you," the Goblin said after a moment. "It involves the vial of serum Spider-Man took from you a few weeks back. Remember that one?"

"Go on," Carnage said. "I'm listening for the moment."

"My idea also involves killing Spider-Man."

"I plan on killing him, with or without you," Carnage said. "But it looks like I will need to search for him." Carnage paused for a moment, then looked at Goblin. "What do you know of that serum?"

"I have it hidden in a very safe place," Goblin said. He patted one of his pumpkin bombs. "And I have a few drops of it right in here, just to drive Spider-Man over the edge."

The woman in Carnage's tentacles struggled and Carnage held her even farther out over the open concrete until she stopped. "Go on, I'm listening."

The Goblin laughed and did a quick circle on his glider in front of the plane door. "I have bait placed for Spider-Man on a bridge near here. Bait he won't be able to withstand."

"Bait? What kind of bait?"

The Goblin laughed and his laugh echoed over the crowds and the police surrounding the plane.

"Anyone ever tell you that your laugh is very annoying?" Carnage said.

"Part of my charm," the Goblin said. And then laughed again.

Carnage waved a few tendrils and a few hundred weapons formed on his body. "Stop that laughing and tell me about the Spider-Man bait."

The Goblin looked around. "I thought I was going to need the bait to draw him away from here, but I underestimated his level of fear. It's an old friend, put in the same position where another old friend was killed years ago."

"You think this *bait* will work?" Carnage asked. "Bring him out in the open?"

"Without a doubt," the Goblin said. "He'll show up there when he knows, which might be any time now. You want to come along for the fun?"

Carnage shrugged. "I was growing tired of airline food. How about a ride?"

"Bring the woman as a shield," Goblin said, swooping in and letting Carnage snag a few tentacles onto the glider. Then in a smooth motion the three of them lifted away from the plane.

At three hundred feet over the crowd, Goblin glanced back at Carnage hanging peacefully behind him and slightly below the glider. The woman was being held by a thin line of red tentacle, being pulled like a tail of a kite. As long as they held her, the cops wouldn't shoot.

Her face was pure white with terror, her eyes huge as she clutched at the thin line of Carnage's skin.

"I think we can lose the luggage," Goblin said once they cleared the airport.

"Thanks for the flight," Carnage said to the woman. Suddenly she dropped away from them toward the crowd below. The mass of people scattered as the woman smashed into a concrete road and bounced.

"Oops," Carnage said. "She slipped."

Their laughter could be heard for miles.

* * *

Subways can be the slowest forms of transportation. After what had seemed like years, Spider-Man had finally gotten off five stations down the line from where he boarded. He figured if the guys in gray suits were this far away, he was going to have to fight his way to the airport. He just didn't have any more time to be riding around on a subway.

He went up the staircase entrance using the ceiling over the people climbing the stairs. His spider-sense told him everything was clear, no gray-suits in sight, at least for the moment.

He was about to hit the nearest building with a web and take off for the airport when a young kid yelled, "There's Spider-Man."

All faces in a crowd of people standing in front of a nearby window full of televisions turned his way.

"Spider-Man," a street vendor called Mort called out. "You need to see this!" He pointed at the window of televisions. "Come quick!"

Mort had been a longtime supporter of Spidey, and he'd been sure to patronize his newsstand both as Peter Parker and Spider-Man.

With a quick jump, Spidey was beside Mort and in the middle of the crowd looking at the window full of televisions. The crowd around them slowly moved a safe distance to each side.

What Spider-Man saw was far worse than the nightmare of blood flowing in the streets.

Carnage was being lowered to the top of one of the Brooklyn Bridge's stone pillars by the Green Goblin.

And on the other side of the same pillar, the very same pillar that Gwen Stacy fell from, was another woman.

As Spider-Man watched the camera pan in closer, his past became his present.

The day Gwen Stacy died mixed in his mind with the images on those twenty television screens in the store window.

The sight of Gwen falling flashed like a strobe light behind his eyes.

The camera panned in even closer on the woman, her face frozen in fear.

Spidey felt his knees go weak under him and he reached out and held onto Mort's shoulder.

"Mary Jane," he said softly.

"You know her?" Mort asked

Spider-Man didn't answer.

A low growl that seemed to come from some place deep inside Spider-Man filled the street.

Mort and the other people close by stepped back.

Spider-Man hit the building above the televisions with a web, and almost quicker than anyone in the crowd could follow, he was headed toward the Brooklyn Bridge.

His nightmare had come true right before his eyes. And he was so tired and so afraid that he couldn't tell exactly what was the past and what was the present in this nightmare.

* * *

The people in front of the window watched for a moment in the direction Spider-Man had disappeared, then turned back to the screens.

Mort turned to the woman in a business dress who moved in beside him and said, ''I think he's really mad.''

The woman glanced again in the direction Spider-Man had gone, then looked at Mort, nodding. ''Yeah, I think Carnage and the green guy with the funky sled have gone and done it now.''

Mort smiled and turned back to the window. ''Get 'em, Spidey.''

And through the rest of the crowd he heard his comment echoed a dozen times.

# CHAPTER (13)

The crisp air of the New York fall day did very little to cool Spider-Man's fear and anger.

In all his life he had never moved as fast as he moved toward the Brooklyn Bridge. He covered the twenty-plus blocks quicker than he had ever dreamed possible, almost yanking himself from one web to the next, using free-fall to speed his swings. Even the flight of the webs shot at the next building seemed too slow for what he wanted.

*Faster. Faster*, he kept repeating to himself. He could feel the sweat covering his face inside his mask and making his hands sticky inside his gloves. But it didn't matter. He had to get there and save Mary Jane.

For most of the twenty blocks he wasn't actually aware of where he was. He was moving on instinct, fear, and not much more. His mind fought the picture he'd seen on the televisions in the store window. Mary Jane, held captive on the top of the Brooklyn Bridge by the Green Goblin. He was so tired, her face kept switching to Gwen's face in his mind.

Then he'd fight Mary Jane's face back to the forefront.

Then Gwen's face would float up.

Gwen. Mary Jane. Like two photographs, one superimposed over the other.

Faster and faster he pushed himself.

Finally, after what seemed like an eternity to Spider-Man, the stone structure and long cables of the Brooklyn Bridge were in sight, stretching across the river to the buildings on the other side.

The stone pillars of the Brooklyn Bridge had an almost Gothic look and contained two arches where the incoming and outgoing traffic passed through. Three huge, metal-encased cables, one on each side, and the third between the two roadways, ran the length of the bridge. Huge concrete pads anchored them into solid rock. The cables disappeared into the stone arches near the top, almost as if they were draped over the arches like a child would drape string over a toy.

Between the stone pillars, the huge cables drooped down to the surface of the road and then climbed back to the top of the next arch. Smaller steel cables ran straight down from the huge supports to the bridge surface.

The three main cables were each as wide in diameter as a sidewalk, but only the top few inches of the slick, weathered surface could be walked on. And near the stone pillars, the cables slanted upward very steeply, making it impossible to climb for any normal human.

Spider-Man forced the thoughts of Gwen from his mind as he swung down off the last building closest to the bridge. The situation he faced didn't look good. Not good at all.

Mary Jane lay on the top of the stone pillar directly over the outbound traffic lanes. Carnage stood a distance away over the incoming traffic. The Green Goblin circled over both of them. Even from this distance Spidey could hear the Goblin's laugh. The same laugh he had used the moment after he knocked Gwen from the same stone pillar.

Spidey couldn't stop his mind from replaying the horror of Gwen falling. He could see her face, looking up at him.

Her blonde hair and gray coat snapping in the wind as she gained speed falling toward the river.

Spidey shook his head. *Come on. Forget that. Save Mary Jane. Do it right this time.*

As Spidey swung toward the base of the bridge, the sun hit the river just right and Spidey swore the surface turned to blood.

Bright red blood.

*Nightmare*, Spidey tried to reassure himself. *This is a nightmare. Wake up! Come on, Spidey. Wake up.*

But it wasn't the type of nightmare he could wake up from. Just as he could never wake up and have Gwen still be alive and laughing.

Ignoring the bloody look of the water, he reached the base of the bridge and started up the cable at full speed. Around him the police had stopped all the traffic on the bridge and were holding the spectators and press back a hundred feet from the on ramps to the bridge. The windows and roofs of all the buildings along the river were full of spectators.

As Spider-Man started up the bridge a huge cheer broke from the surrounding crowd and grew, echoing through the buildings and over the bridge.

But Spidey paid no attention. His only focus was simple and single-tracked. *Get Mary Jane off of there.*

*Alive.*

"Well, well, well," Carnage said as Spidey neared the stone pillar. "Our guest of honor has arrived."

The Goblin only laughed. Then, putting his glider into a steep dive, he went directly at Spider-Man, firing sparkle beams from his glove as he went.

Spidey danced along the top of the cable, easily avoiding the exploding beams. As the Goblin passed, Spidey simply ducked under the edge of the glider and kept moving for the top.

''I think you missed him,'' Carnage yelled out at the Goblin, laughing.

The Goblin swung up over the top of the stone and came in straight, meaning to hit Spider-Man as he jumped from the cable to the top of the stone pillar.

But Spidey's spider-sense warned of the attack and he rolled sideways as the Goblin flashed past. The glider clipped Spider-Man's heel.

Spidey came to his feet facing Carnage.

The red and black monster stood on the other side of the stone pillar, not making a move at Spidey. It seemed for the moment he was enjoying the fight between Spider-Man and the Green Goblin too much to interfere.

''Close one, but no cigar,'' Carnage said, again laughing.

The Goblin let out a long, hard laugh as he took the glider around the top of the pillar in a tight turn. The laugh designed by Norman Osborn to drive his enemies insane with its very sound.

''I wish you wouldn't do that,'' Carnage said, covering his ears. ''It's annoying beyond belief.''

Spidey could see that his wife was alive and bound with her arms behind her back and her feet tied. Her eyes were wide in fear.

Gwen hadn't been tied. She had simply been unconscious. Spidey hadn't paid enough attention to the Goblin when he went to Gwen on top the bridge and the Goblin had knocked her off the edge, almost right out of his arms. Spidey wouldn't give him the same chance this time.

He made a quick, "stay down" motion to Mary Jane with his hand and then focused back on the Goblin. He wouldn't have the time to get her off this pillar without a diversion first. The man in the Goblin suit seemed to be the logical choice.

The Goblin was coming in from downriver, firing sparkle beams that pitted the top of the bridge around Spider-Man's feet.

"You're an awful shot," Spidey said as the Goblin came on straight. He was obviously going to try to ram Spider-Man.

"We'll see who's laughing last," the Goblin said.

"Very original," Spidey said as he stepped aside, letting the glider brush past him. Then, when the Goblin pulled the glider into a climb Spidey fired two webs. One hit the Goblin in the back of his purple vest, and the other web caught the glider.

Spidey quickly stuck his end of web on the glider to the edge of the pillar.

He braced his feet as best he could on the flat concrete surface and just before the web line attached to the glider went tight he yanked on the line attached to the Goblin.

Hard.

The Goblin came off the glider with a grunt, his legs flying up over his head. The glider hit the end of the web and the web held. The glider instantly went into a dive, headed for the river, the web line pulling it like a kite on a string as its own power kept it accelerating downward.

After it was clear the Goblin's glider was going to power straight into the river, Spidey let go of the web, and in one motion had Mary Jane over his shoulder and headed down the cable toward the edge of the bridge.

Behind him, Carnage sprang into action. A large knife formed on his arm and spun off at the web line dragging the glider in a sharp dive at the river. The knife sliced the line as the Goblin fell past the top of the pillar toward the river.

Carnage watched as the Goblin turned over in midair and punched the homing device for the glider.

The glider righted itself and did a quick loop, ending up diving at the river at a faster pace than the Goblin, but above him. The two came together a hundred feet over the water, and at ten feet over the water the Goblin was remounted and had the glider moving horizontally.

Far above, Carnage applauded. "Nicely done," he shouted.

Spider-Man reached the bottom of the bridge and went quickly into the crowd. The people moved aside like waves and then closed in behind him, giving him some visual shelter from his two enemies above him.

He stood Mary Jane up and then with a quick snap broke her ropes away.

"Are you all right?"

Mary Jane nodded, her face obviously flushed. "Yes."

Spider-Man leaned in close to her and whispered, "I love you."

Then without waiting for a response, he turned and jumped over the crowd between him and the bridge. He had a debt to settle. No one kidnapped his wife and got away with it.

No one.

He was furious. And some of the anger still came from Gwen's death. And some came from being so tired and frustrated. But most of it came from these two lunatics kidnapping his wife.

He was angry and someone was going to pay.

Carnage stood on the stone pillar and the Green Goblin circled overhead.

Spidey knew without a doubt that whoever wore the Goblin costume today was no Osborn. Both Norman and Harry had a toughness and a real style to them when they were the Green Goblin. This guy could handle the glider, but not much else. And he had no style and very little strength. However, teamed with Carnage, and armed with the Goblin's arsenal, he was still dangerous.

As Spider-Man mounted the huge bridge cable and ran for the top, another huge cheer filled the air as hundreds of people shouted their support.

"My, but aren't you a popular fellow," Carnage said from the top of the pillar as Spider-Man approached.

Spidey stopped on the center cable between the traffic lanes, just out of reach of Carnage's longest tentacles. "Wait until you hear them cheer when I knock you and your phony sidekick into the river."

"I'm afraid they'll never get the chance," Carnage said.

Spidey felt his spider-sense warn him as the Goblin stopped circling and dove, firing sparkle beams.

Spidey jumped to the top of the next cable and easily out of the way as the Goblin went diving past.

"Who is the clown?" Spider-Man asked, indicating the Green Goblin who tried to turn the glider quickly for another pass at Spidey.

"Entertaining, isn't he?" Carnage said. "But he claims

to have some of Catrall's serum in one of his pumpkin bombs.''

For a moment everything around Spidey went numb. Two weeks of worrying and having nightmares over who stole the deadly serum and now the nightmare had just gotten worse. This so-called Green Goblin, teamed with Carnage, had the serum. And if Carnage had his way, the streets of New York really would be flowing in blood.

Spidey shook his head and glanced at where the Goblin had climbed back into the air above him. ''I don't believe you.''

''You should always believe a man dressed like Carnage,'' the Goblin said. And then he laughed, the Green Goblin laugh.

''Would you stop that laugh!'' Carnage shouted. ''I warned you.''

''So the team is bickering,'' Spidey said.

''We're not a team,'' Carnage said.

''Except when it comes to killing you,'' the Goblin said.

Spidey glanced at the Goblin who had circled and now hovered on his glider facing down the cable. In his hand was a pumpkin bomb.

''Toss it in the crowd,'' Carnage said. ''It will be so much fun to see Spider-Man trying to rescue a thousand people who have all gone mad at once.''

''No,'' the Goblin said. ''This is for Spider-Man.'' With a quick overhand throw the Goblin launched the pumpkin bomb directly at Spidey.

Spidey figured the best plan he had was keep the bomb from exploding, or explode it over the river where the wind would disperse the serum. He aimed his web-shooters at the bomb flying at him. He was only going to get one chance at this. He better hit the shot perfectly, or he was going to get a quick test of Dr. Catrall's serum.

But Carnage had other ideas.

Carnage caught the bomb in midair with a tentacle, and with a quick flip launched the bomb into a high arc.

The bomb headed in a direct line at the crowds at the end of the bridge.

"No!" Spider-Man shouted. Mary Jane was in that crowd somewhere.

But there was nothing he could do.

The bomb was out of his reach or the reach of his best web shot.

The three of them watched as the orange bomb seemed to take forever to reach the ground.

# CHAPTER (14)

Mary Jane moved to a place in the middle of the crowd staring at the Brooklyn Bridge where she could see. No one paid her any attention. A moment before she had been at the center of their interest. Now, with the scene on the bridge, she was forgotten and she was happy for that.

Spider-Man had gone back up the steel cable toward the Green Goblin and Carnage. Now he stood on the cable facing the two enemies, his back to the crowd. For the moment they seemed to be talking.

She rubbed her wrists where the rope had cut and bruised them. Peter had snapped the ropes like they were so much tissue. Yet with her he was always so tender.

Standing here, with thousands who were cheering for him, she got a glimpse of what he did for others. Sometimes she saw it on television; other times in the newspaper. But usually he never talked about what he had done and she doubted it ever occurred to him to brag. He drove himself for weeks without sleep, risking his life simply because he wanted to save lives and help others. Nothing more.

It seemed that no one, except the few like Peter, seemed to want to take responsibility for their own actions. It was fashionable to blame whoever or whatever was handy when something went wrong. She had never heard Peter blame anyone or anything but himself. Usually he took too much responsibility. But she'd rather have him doing that than whining around the apartment feeling sorry for himself all the time.

"I love you," she whispered at her husband on the bridge.

Then she clenched her hands together in front of her and tried to swallow the fear building inside. She desperately wanted to run, get away from here and the fight she knew was coming. But if Peter could do his job and face these two, the least she could do was try to stay calm.

And stay beside him, at least in spirit.

* * *

K.L. Bogal heard of the situation developing at the Brooklyn Bridge from a police radio broadcast. The minute the name Carnage was mentioned, he knew Spider-Man would be there.

He shouted orders through the basement headquarters and within five minutes all fifty of his men were loaded into vans. Each had been issued a stun rifle. Bogal figured that Spider-Man could stand a fall from the Brooklyn Bridge into the water even if one of his men got trigger happy. But he had still given all his men a strict warning to not fire unless he ordered it. Then with sirens blaring on the vans, they fought their way through traffic to City Hall, which was as close to the bridge as they could get.

As they double-timed it on foot the last two blocks to the entrance to the bridge, Bogal could see Spider-Man coming down the cable at full speed carrying a woman in his arms. On the top of the bridge Carnage stood intently watching as another man fell toward the river.

"The Green Goblin," one of his men said as the falling man was caught by a jet-powered sled that looked more like a bat than anything.

"I hope we're not too late," Bogal muttered to himself.

If Spider-Man didn't come back, they'd have to go back to tracking him in the city. And after the events of this morning, Bogal wasn't sure that was such a good idea. Lifestream Technologies had a lot of contacts in the city and state governments and could pull a lot of strings. But covering up a thousand people suddenly getting dizzy and fainting was hard to do.

A moment later Spider-Man scampered back up the cable to a point below Carnage. There he stopped.

"Now just stay there for a moment," Bogal said.

He shoved forward to the police blockade. "Federal agent," he said, showing an actual FBI badge. He hadn't asked how Lifestream had come to have the badge, but the picture of him matched and that was all that mattered.

Bogal turned and pointed to his men in gray suits carrying stun rifles. "We need to get into position to help Spider-Man."

The cops on the blockade scampered to let Bogal and his men through. He could feel the wind at his back as he directed his men to move twenty feet in front of the crowd and then spread out over two lanes. Then he looked up to watch the action above.

"Get ready to fire," he shouted to his men. "Set on wide beam."

As a unit they snapped the stun rifles to their shoulders, kneeled, and aimed at the bridge. That many rifles at once would take down not only Spider-Man, but Carnage and the Goblin. He would be considered a hero by the city.

Suddenly there was a flurry of action on the top of the bridge and an orange ball was floating in the air toward him.

"What in the world is—"

The pumpkin bomb exploded right behind Bogal and right in the middle of his men.

Twenty feet behind them the crowd and the cops shoved backward, keeping out of the small cloud forming from the explosion. The wind continued to blow slightly offshore and out over the water, which was lucky for the crowd.

But Bogal and all his men were not so fortunate.

Bogal's ears were ringing as he was covered by the mist. He shook his head, trying to clear it.

Then he realized what he had to do.

He could feel the anger welling up inside him. He hated everything and everyone. He never got the respect he deserved and he was going to show them all right now.

A low growl escaped from his throat.

He stepped toward his nearest man and with a quick snap broke the man's neck.

And doing that only made him angrier.

* * *

Spider-Man could feel the panic and the helplessness almost overwhelm him as the pumpkin bomb flew beyond his reach toward the crowd below.

Then he saw where it was going to fall.

The men in the gray suits were kneeling on the bridge, all pointing rifles at him. They had been about to knock him and Carnage and the Green Goblin into the river with their disorienting stun guns. No wonder his spider-sense had been going off. He'd been so tired, he just figured it was because of Carnage and the Green Goblin. Logical assumption when he thought about it.

The pumpkin bomb hit square in the middle of the men

and exploded, filling the air around them with a cloud. The people and the cops behind them surged back, out of the way. If Mary Jane was in that crowd, she would be safe for the moment.

The cloud drifted almost at once low out over the river and started to disperse, but it had covered all the men in gray suits.

"Nice shot," Carnage said, "don't you think?"

"That was for Spider-Man," the Goblin roared.

Carnage shrugged. "He'll be dead soon, so what does it matter?"

Below, the men in gray suits started to move. A few crouched low. A few others simply stood and shook their heads.

Then one man turned, went back to one of his men, and broke the guy's neck in one quick twist.

Suddenly the inbound lanes of the Brooklyn Bridge became a killing field. Guns forgotten, the men went at each other like animals. Biting, clawing, hitting, they ripped each other apart.

Ten of the men in gray tackled the first guy, swarming over him like ants over a dead animal. The guy fought a good fight, ripping apart two of his men, but within seconds he had a broken leg.

Six men stood around him, kicking him. After a moment he lay still and the men turned on each other.

The crowd on the street stood in silent shock watching. All attention to the three on the bridge was lost as the bloodbath continued. Finally, the ten cops along the line holding people off the bridge stepped forward, guns drawn and ordered the fighting to stop.

But the gray-suited men paid no notice. They continued

to kill each other until there were only five of them left standing. Then, blood dripping from them, they turned to the cops, who had now drawn their weapons.

Spider-Man heard one cop shout, "Stop!" as the men started toward them.

"Stop right there!" another shouted, and all ten cops backed up a step, never taking their gaze from the gray-suited men advancing on them.

Finally the advance had gone too far and the crowd behind was in danger. One cop pointed his gun at one man's knees and fired. The man went down and then kept crawling at the cops, saliva dripping from his mouth.

Other cops opened fire and within a few seconds the last of the gray-suited men lay bleeding on the pavement. As the last echoes of the gunfire faded and was gone, a horrified silence covered the thousands watching. Never, not even during the dead of night, had this section of New York been this silent.

Spider-Man refused to believe what he had just seen. The bridge was littered with bodies. The blood reflected the sunlight like red mirrors. His nightmares had been right. If Dr. Catrall's serum ever got into a public water supply, the streets of New York really would run in rivers of blood.

Carnage broke the silence with a laugh of glee. "That was *fantastic*! We need to go get more of that stuff."

Spider-Man turned around, forcing himself to take his gaze off the bloodbath below. Carnage had been talking to the Green Goblin.

The Goblin laughed. "There is much more where that came from. Much more."

Spider-Man, the nightmare flashing through his mind

like a flickering video, jumped up onto the top of the stone pillar and turned toward Carnage. Carnage and this impostor Goblin could never be allowed to reach that serum.

Never.

Spider-Man took a deep breath. "Let's finish this. I'm tired of looking at your two ugly faces."

# CHAPTER (15)

The attack from Carnage was almost instantaneous. Knives formed on his arms and spun off at Spider-Man almost faster than Spider-Man could see them.

With a quick dive, knives slashing through he air around him, he was off the edge of the stone pillar. He went down to the huge cable and swung under it as the rain of knives followed him, ringing like hail off the cable's metal casing. Spidey could feel that his reaction time was just a fraction slow from being so tired. He'd have to be careful.

The Green Goblin's laugh echoed off the river and the road below.

"Thought you wanted to fight," Carnage said where he stood on the side of the stone pillar.

The Goblin laughed again and Carnage looked up at where the green and purple villain hovered on his glider. Barbs and spears formed and dissolved and then reformed on Carnage's arms, clearly showing he wasn't happy. "I *told* you to cut out that laugh!"

Spider-Man used Carnage's short distraction with the Goblin to swing unnoticed through the traffic arch and go quickly up the other side of the stone pillar.

As he jumped up on top, Carnage was glancing again over the edge where Spider-Man used to be.

"You going to hide down there all day?" Carnage snickered.

Using both web-shooters, Spidey aimed at the back of Carnage's head and fired a baseball-sized glob of hardening web. The webs caught Carnage like a sledgehammer square in the back of his head. Since he was already leaning forward, the force of the blow sent him tumbling out into the air.

Carnage must have been stunned by the blow because he did five complete tumbles before he managed to send out a tendril and snag the edge of the roadway to stop his fall all the way to the river. As the tendril stopped him, Spidey could see Carnage's body yank up short, like a bungie-jumper hitting the end of a rope that had no spring to it.

"Yow, that must have hurt," Spidey said.

"Die!" the Goblin said as he dove his glider at Spidey. At the same time the Goblin fired sparkle beam after sparkle beam.

Spidey easily sidestepped the beams as they exploded around him, and then he landed a glancing right cross to the Goblin's head as he passed.

It hadn't been that hard a blow and either of the Osborn Green Goblins wouldn't have even noticed it. But this Goblin did a few spirals over the water before he righted the glider and started back at Spidey.

His spider-sense warned him that Carnage was coming back up the tower at him. Spidey glanced over the edge at the red and black monster swarming up the cables of the bridge.

Fifty spears flew at Spidey from Carnage's arms, and Spidey ducked back, rolling out of the way of the next pass of the Goblin.

The Goblin also had to swerve quickly to keep from getting run through by the spears. Again he did a few out-of-control spirals before he got the sled going level again.

"You guys are going to have to practice together

more," Spidey said, backing away from the edge as Carnage came over the top. "Your timing is way off."

Off to one side, Spidey could see that the Goblin now had a pumpkin bomb in his hand. Spidey hoped this one was just a normal exploding one like Norman and Harry used to use. If it was, maybe he could use it to his advantage.

Carnage looked like a moving armory. Knives, spears, barbed hooks, needles, all formed and then melted on his arms and chest as his black and red skin continuously flowed and moved.

Spidey was about ten steps from Carnage.

The Goblin was making another run, pumpkin bomb held high over his head, ready to throw.

Spidey waited for just an instant, then took a step forward at Carnage.

A dozen or more needle-knives flashed from Carnage at Spidey.

Spidey dropped to the concrete and rolled toward Carnage. Then quickly coming up, he stepped inside Carnage's flying tentacles and landed the hardest punch he could throw on Carnage's chin.

The punch rocked Spider-Man to his very tired core and sent Carnage end over end toward the edge of the stone pillar.

Spidey's spider-sense warned him that the Goblin was almost in range to throw the bomb.

Quickly Spidey stepped toward the stunned Carnage and hit him on the side of the head, again as hard as he could. A sharp stab of pain shot through Spidey's arm. Too many more like that blow and he'd break his hand. That wouldn't make much difference. He was so tired, he didn't have many more of those punches left in his arm.

Then his spider-sense went off like an alarm and he jumped high and backwards, flipping twice in the air before he landed on the concrete.

The pumpkin bomb hit right where he had been, right next to the slowly rising and very angry Carnage.

The explosion sent Carnage doing backflips again toward the river far below. The Goblin couldn't believe what he had done and almost didn't pull his glider up in time to avoid slamming into the concrete surface.

Spidey got to the edge just in time to see Carnage again manage at the last minute to snag a support structure on the roadway, and stop his long fall to the very hard water. Again Spidey could see Carnage bounce from the jolt of the sudden stop.

Spidey glanced around at the Goblin. "Nice job. But I tell you, he's going to be *really* mad when he gets back up here."

The Goblin again shouted, "Die!" and dove for Spider-Man, shooting sparkle beams.

"Boy, you need to work on your fight patter," Spidey said, doing a slight dance sideways to stay out of the way of the poorly-aimed beams. "Didn't they teach you anything in villain school?"

Again the Goblin tried to ram Spidey with his pointed glider, but the wall-crawler easily moved aside and the Goblin went flying off into the air over the river. The guy in the Goblin suit knew how to handle the machinery, but not much more than that. And he didn't have Norman or Harry's enhanced strength. As tired as Spidey was, that was a very lucky break.

Spidey glanced over the side. Carnage was over halfway back and moving faster than Spidey could remember Kasady ever moving. "How you doing down there?"

Carnage said nothing as bloodlike saliva dripped from his teeth.

*I think you've really pissed him off now, Spidey old fella.* Quickly, Spider-Man went to the other side of the stone pillar and dropped down over the side, figuring he'd try to come up behind Carnage again.

He was wrong. And if he hadn't been so tired he'd have known the same thing never worked twice in a row with Carnage.

Just as Spidey dropped off the edge his spider-sense went wild. Before Spidey could stop his drop, Carnage came out from under the pillar and caught him with a hard sledgehammer punch in the stomach.

Spidey exhaled as if trying to blow out candles on a cake from fifty feet. And then he couldn't breathe at all.

The wind was knocked out of him. The only thing he could see was the world spinning end over end. At least it wasn't spinning around and around like it had earlier this morning. He didn't think his stomach could handle that again so soon.

Spreading his arms and legs so that he slowed his spin through the air, he figured out where the nearest cable was and fired a web. So it was his turn to be knocked off the tower, as if the two of them were playing King of the Mountain or something.

The web caught and he swung smoothly over the incoming lanes toward the middle cable.

Then his spider-sense really went wild.

The Goblin, grinning like a fool and laughing like a hyena, was coming in from Spidey's right, firing sparkle beams out of both gloves like a machine gun.

Above and to the left, Carnage was launching spears like they too were machine gun bullets.

And Spidey was swinging right into the crossfire.

He let the web he was swinging on go and fell toward the bridge surface. Then he fired another web downward at a support cable and yanked on the web hard, almost dislocating his shoulder, but sending him hurtling ten times as fast at the bridge.

That move barely got him out of the crossfire.

With another web shot, he caught a cable on the center support and then held on for dear life as his speed nearly yanked his arm out of its socket.

But he missed the road by ten feet, swinging out over the water. He let go again, then spun around and hit the guardrail of the bridge with a web and swung back underneath.

He caught a beam there and hung on, trying for the first time in what seemed like years to breathe. The breaths came slow and shuddering, but he finally got his stomach muscles and lungs to work together and he took in some air.

But his spider-sense told him trouble was coming.

The Goblin did a high banking turn out over the water and made a run at Spidey's position under the bridge, firing sparkle beams as he came.

Spidey moved his shoulder around for a moment, making sure he could still use it after the jolt. Then he moved quickly up behind a huge support beam under the bridge, and as the Goblin made his run firing at where Spidey had last been, Spidey timed his jump and landed squarely on the back of the Goblin.

"Taxi?" Spidey asked. He had pulled this maneuver on the original Goblin once or twice, but rarely with any success.

This Goblin quickly lost control of the glider. They did three quick spins while still under the bridge. Finally, with Spidey's help, the Goblin got them righted and over the water.

Spidey quickly covered the Goblin's eyes with webbing.

"You'll kill us both," the Goblin said, frantically scraping at this blindfold.

Spidey used his knees on the Goblin's back to force him to turn the glider and climb back toward the top of the stone pillar. "I steer, you just push on the gas."

Carnage had moved halfway down the center cable and now stood watching.

Spidey waved at him as they climbed past.

Spidey steered the Goblin so the glider would just miss the top of the pillar, then when they were over the flat top he jumped off and let the Goblin and the glider go on.

"Thanks for the lift."

Still clawing at the webbing in his eyes, the Goblin continued in a fairly straight line up and away, the jets from the glider pushing him like a rocket.

Spidey laughed. "He doesn't get that stuff off soon, he'll be in orbit."

Spidey turned as Carnage came back up over the opposite edge of the pillar.

"You think you're so funny, don't you?" Carnage asked, his body rippling with anger.

Spidey shrugged. "My fans think I do a pretty good stand-up. Why, don't you?"

"They laugh at a jerk."

Spidey grabbed his chest and pretended to stagger. "Ouch, now that hurt me."

"I'll do more than just hurt you," Carnage said, firing twenty spears at Spidey as he rushed forward.

Spidey jumped over the spears and then rolled sideways out of the way of a hail of knives off Carnage's body.

"Didn't like the routine, huh?" Spidey said, landing in front Carnage. Carnage swiped at Spidey with razor-edged tentacles.

Spidey twisted inside, narrowly missed getting cut, and then landed another punch on Carnage's chin. "There's always a critic in every crowd."

The punch tired Spidey even more and only sent Carnage staggering back a few steps. This was going to have to end soon or Spidey was going to be in real trouble.

Spider-Man backed off as Carnage took a deep breath, obviously attempting to clear the effects of Spidey's punch. Over the river and about five hundred feet above the bridge, the Goblin had managed to clear his eyes. He had turned the glider and was heading back toward the top of the pillar at top speed.

Spidey moved around so his back was to the Goblin. He had an idea how to end this, straight out of his own nightmare. But to make it work it was going to take perfect timing.

"Getting kind of weak-kneed, aren't you?" Spidey said, taunting Carnage.

"You want weak knees?" Knives formed around both of Carnage's knees and fired at Spidey almost faster than he could see it happening. Spidey jumped, but one of the knives sliced across his leg.

The Spidey rolled, ducking more knives thrown off Carnage's arms.

"You're not going to have much body left at that rate," Spidey said, keeping his back directly on the Goblin. His spider-sense told him the Goblin was getting closer and closer.

"More than enough to kill you," Carnage said.

"You think so?" Spidey said, moving another step closer to Carnage. At this point they were less than ten feet apart, both half-crouched like two fighters in a ring, waiting for the other to make the next move.

Spidey could tell that Carnage saw the Goblin coming. And Carnage was expecting the Goblin to just ram Spidey.

Spider-Man's spider-sense warning was screaming in his head. But he had to wait. Wait until the very last second.

Wait.

Wait.

Now. It was time to act.

Faster than the normal human eye could follow, Spider-Man hit Carnage in the face with two web shots, covering his eyes and momentarily blinding him. At the same time Spidey jumped as high and as hard as his tired legs would let him.

The Goblin and his glider missed Spidey's heels by less than a foot, and rammed directly into Carnage, catching the red-and-black killer square in the stomach with the point of the bat-shaped glider.

The collision, the glider still on full power, sent Carnage and the Goblin over the edge of the pillar at a downward angle. The Goblin had thought he could ram Spidey in the back and push him into the river. Both the Osborn Green Goblins had tried that same stunt numbers of times and they never really got it to work either. This Goblin should have studied a little history.

In the air over them Spidey hit the Goblin in the back with a web and yanked. The yank was enough to pull the Goblin from the glider, but it also sent Spidey slamming into the stone top of the pillar.

At the last moment he managed to stop himself from being pulled right off the edge as he held onto the web with the Goblin. He ended up hanging over the edge, watching the Goblin below.

The web was long enough that the Goblin swung down under the stone arch. As he was about ten feet off the surface of the inbound lanes of highway, the Goblin twisted around and managed to cut the web holding him. The Goblin dropped and rolled on the pavement.

Then he was up and running, headed for the end of the bridge and the city beyond.

*Only one shot*, Spidey thought as he shot a spider-tracer at the back of the Goblin. The tracer stuck near the Goblin's shoulder and the Goblin didn't seem to notice as he jumped over the bodies of the guys in gray suits. The Goblin fired a few sparkle beams at the pavement and the police and the crowd scattered, letting him through.

"I'll deal with you later," Spider-Man said. At the moment Carnage was much, much more important than some Goblin impostor, even though the impostor had Catrall's serum.

Spidey got to his feet and looked down toward the river

as the Goblin glider, still accelerating, smashed Carnage into the water.

The impact sent a huge spray, and both Carnage and the glider disappeared under the surface in a bubbling rush.

Then the water slowly calmed and all was silent.

Spidey hit the big cable below him with a web and swung down. In only a moment he was hanging by a web ten feet over the water, searching, waiting for any sign of Carnage. Finally, about twenty feet away the body of Cletus Kasady floated to the surface.

He was out cold and looked dead. There was no sign of his living costume.

Spidey hit him with a web and then, using what seemed to be the last of his strength, he hauled the body back to the surface of the bridge.

There he was met by twenty police and ten others dressed in Vault Guardsmen uniforms.

Spidey rolled the body of Kasady over and looked at his face. For a moment he thought he was dead. But then Kasady took in a shallow, shuddering breath. The guy was hurt, of that there was no doubt. The glider must have driven him into that river at over two hundred miles per hour. Carnage only survived because he was protected by his alien outfit. But it didn't look like he was going to be any trouble to anyone for a while.

The Guardsmen were taking no chances, however. They took his arms and pulled them out wide, hooking them so that no matter what happened, he couldn't scratch himself and become Carnage again. Three others were quickly setting up an electrically charged portable cell.

They'd have him back inside the Vault in a matter of

a few hours' flight. For the moment, Carnage was not a problem.

Spidey took a deep breath and stood. But he still had a vial of deadly serum to find and a Goblin impostor to unmask. He couldn't rest just yet, no matter what his body told him it needed.

At a run, he headed toward the end of the bridge.

And as he did, the dozens along the water and the roads and the hundreds more in the windows of the buildings applauded and cheered.

And Spidey took it in as much as he could, using their energy and good thoughts to give him enough strength to finish this battle and come out on top.

He reached the side of the bridge and hit a nearby building with a web, pulling himself into the air and into the city.

\* \* \*

Below him, Mary Jane watched her tired and beat-up husband swing off. Right at that moment she was as proud of him as she had ever been.

"Come home soon," she whispered.

# CHAPTER (16)

 Spider-Man followed the trail of the spider-tracer across town. His muscles ached and his mind felt like it was full of mush. He forced himself to take deep breaths of the crisp fall air to clear his head. Then he concentrated on hitting the correct spot with each web, letting the swing through the air be time to rest.

As he had figured it might, the tracer led him back to the abandoned building across from the old Osborn headquarters. And then down under the building.

Spidey went in a broken side window on the second floor. The unbroken windows were so coated in dirt that the inside was gloomy and many places very dark. The place had been a set of offices once and phone jacks stuck out of the walls like the stubble of a bum's beard. Squares of bright paint marked where paintings used to hang. The floor was covered with trash and dirt. Rat droppings were scattered everywhere like pepper on a salad.

Moving as quietly as the creaking floors of the old building would let him, he moved down the fire stairs, past the first floor and into the multiple basements of the building.

The first two basements were an abandoned parking garage. In New York, that space alone was worth millions. The third basement down housed utility rooms and storage. A maze of corridors and small rooms wound through the dark. He let the tracer lead him in the mostly dark halls.

Finally, in what seemed to be a long hall, the tracer

told him he needed to turn left, but there was no corridor going left.

"Got you," Spidey said softly to himself.

Behind that wall there must be another of Norman Osborn's stashes of equipment. The guy had gone so crazy and paranoid in his last year that he had scattered his equipment through a lot of his buildings, keeping it behind secret walls and in secret labs. It had been a habit of his that Spidey had paid for many times since Norman Osborn died.

Spider-Man felt along what looked to be a normal block wall, looking for any sign of entry. He finally found the clue he needed on the floor. In the faint light he could see footprints in the dust that disappeared at the wall in one place only.

Spidey took a deep breath and pushed, and the wall moved inward silently.

The light caused him to pause for just a moment, then his eyes adjusted to the lamp. Behind the wall was an old study, filled with books and a desk. On the desk was something Spidey thought he might never see again.

The vial with Dr. Catrall's serum.

Another door stood open on the other side of the office. It looked like it led into a much bigger, almost warehouse-sized space. It seemed to be lit by one bright light off to one side.

His spider-sense told him that the tracer was in there. And so was the Goblin.

Spidey moved silently to the desk, took the vial and moved it to the top of one of the bookshelves. He carefully put the vial behind a few books and replaced the books, being very careful not to disturb the dust on them at all. No one could tell the books had been moved or that he had climbed up there. No one would find it now and it would be out of the Goblin's grasp.

He jumped back to the floor, a sense of relief flooding over him. The visions of rivers of blood flowing through the streets filled his mind, but then suddenly the vision seemed to dry up, as if his action had shut off the blood.

Spidey blinked the vision away. The serum was safe and hidden for the moment. Another problem down and only one more to go. Time to deal with that last problem.

Who was doing the bad Goblin impression?

Spidey moved silently into the warehouse room. The Goblin stood with his back to Spidey, furiously trying to get another Goblin glider to work.

"Might need gas," Spidey said.

The Goblin jumped and spun around.

"Sorry to surprise you," Spidey said.

"How—"

Spidey held up his hand. "Trade secret. But I think it's time you reveal your trade secret, don't you?"

"You're going to die, Spider-Man."

Spidey shook his head. "Like I said, you've got to work on your snappy patter. Maybe get some lessons while you're in jail."

The Goblin still had on one glove and the mask. He stared, almost stunned, at Spider-Man then fired a sparkle-beam.

In these close quarters, he was a lot better shot than he had been on the bridge.

And Spidey was just that much more tired and that much slower. The exploding beam nicked him and he tumbled sideways and came up rolling.

He quickly ducked inside two other sparkle beams, and with a sharp uppercut hit the Goblin solidly in the chin.

The punch lifted the Goblin completely off the floor and back on top of the workbench beside a glider.

"See what happens when you can't patter?" Spidey said.

The Goblin twisted around and fired a sparkle beam at Spidey at closer range.

It barely missed, and the only reason it did was that Spidey jumped hard, doing a high backflip away from the Goblin and the workbench. *Thank goodness for my spider-sense*, he thought, not for the first time.

As Spidey landed fifteen feet away, the Goblin whirled and grabbed a pumpkin bomb from the wall over the bench. Before Spidey could even move, the Goblin had thrown it.

Spidey jumped sideways as the Goblin grabbed another bomb off the desk and threw it.

And then another and another.

The explosions in the abandoned warehouse were as loud as that bomb at Cape Canaveral that Spidey had prevented from destroying a space shuttle. Much louder than anything Spidey could remember hearing in a long time. His ears rang and the concussion knocked him around like a pinball.

And then there was the dust.

The years of dust that had covered every square inch of the room had all been stirred and shaken by the first explosion, and the succeeding ones did nothing but fill the air with a choking, swirling cloud of dust.

In less than ten seconds, Spidey couldn't see a thing.

Suddenly his spider-sense went wild. He jumped

straight up, firing a web at the ceiling to pull himself up even farther.

More explosions rocked the room, one right where he had been standing, making Spidey's ears ring.

The Goblin threw bomb after bomb and just kept throwing them at different places in the room. It was amazing that the force of the explosions didn't bring the old building down on top of both of them.

At one point, hanging from the ceiling, Spidey started to say something smart like, "Missed me!" but then clamped his mouth shut. No point in giving the guy a target when he seemed to have unlimited ammunition.

Spidey lost count at ten explosions, but he guessed, hanging from the ceiling that there were at least fourteen. Maybe one or two more.

The room had been lit with a lamp over the workbench. Now, with the place choked with swirling dust, it was almost pitch black.

Then silence filled the room as the explosions stopped. The sudden silence left Spidey's ears ringing like an alarm. He could tell that the tracer was still in the room, over by the workbench. But he felt no sense of anyone else.

Whoever had been wearing the tracer must have taken off the Goblin costume while he was tossing the bombs. He was probably already out the door.

Making a wild guess in the swirling black dust where the door was, Spidey swung down.

He missed by five feet to the left, avoiding running into the wall only by virtue of his spider-sense. Quickly, he felt his way along until he found the door.

The dust had also poured into the office area, but there

had been more light in there, so Spidey could see the footprints on the floor heading for the open hidden door. There was no sign at all that the Goblin had found or disturbed where Spidey had hidden the deadly serum.

At full speed, he was out the door and heading up the stairs. The guy was ahead of him, two flights up at the street door.

It felt like forever as Spidey went up the stairs, but it was actually only a matter of seconds. The door to the sidewalk was just closing as Spidey burst through and into the bright light.

"Ouch," Spidey said, instantly covering his eyes while trying to look around. It took his eyes just a few seconds to adjust. Then it took him another few seconds to spot who he was looking for on the sidewalk, moving away as fast as possible.

And as Spidey watched, the man with a dust-covered white shirt and black pants changed his shape, slipping into the shape of a woman wearing a purple dress.

The Chameleon.

The man imitating the Goblin and Norman Osborn had been the Chameleon, master of disguise. Of course. If Spidey hadn't been so tired he'd have figured that out. It was the Chameleon who stole the vial and it was the Chameleon who had set Carnage free.

Suddenly it all made sense, like all the pieces of a big puzzle coming together.

Dmitri Smerdyakov, a.k.a. the Chameleon, still blamed Spider-Man for the death of Kraven the Hunter, even though Kraven had killed himself. The Chameleon had looked up to Kraven, had been his servant over the years. And they shared a common enemy in Spider-Man. In fact, the Chameleon was one of the first foes Spidey had ever faced.

Smerdyakov had had his face altered to be void and had developed clothing material that could change with his thoughts. Simply by thinking, he could change into a completely different person—face, clothes, and all—in less than a second.

Spidey started after the Chameleon, trying his best to keep the "woman" in his sights. But the crowds on the sidewalk made it tough, so Spidey jumped to the side of the building and moved along there.

After a moment the Chameleon switched again, becoming a man in a brown business suit. Then he shoved his way into a busy doorway of an office building, letting the circular door swallow him.

Spidey was less than two seconds behind him, but by the time Spidey dropped off the building and got inside the Chameleon had changed again, probably making the shift as he left the door.

And this time Spidey hadn't been able to watch the change. He had no idea who he had changed into.

Spidey stopped and studied everyone he could see, watching their actions closely.

Nothing. Not one clue as to where the guy had gone. No one seemed to be running, or even looking scared.

Spidey scampered up the wall of the office lobby until he was about ten feet over everyone's heads. Then he shouted, "Hey everyone! Attention please!"

The crowd quickly stopped and turned to stare up at Spider-Man.

"Chameleon, I know you can hear me."

Spidey watched the crowd, but no one bolted and ran.

"I will come after you. You are warned."

Spidey watched the crowd for another few long seconds and then nodded to everyone. "Thanks."

He dropped to the floor and was out the door in a flash. There was no way he could catch the Chameleon in that kind of crowd. He had lost him for the moment.

But at least *the* Goblin hadn't returned. That was a huge relief. He hadn't been going insane at all. He'd figure out a way to go after the Chameleon later. But at the moment Spidey still had some loose ends to clean up.

# EPILOGUE

 Spidey swung quickly over the few blocks to the roof of the *Daily Bugle*. This time his spider-sense stayed quiet, so obviously no one was watching. No gray-suited guys with weird helmets and guns trying to knock him out of the sky and following his every movement. It felt great, almost like he'd been let out of jail.

He ducked behind the air conditioning ducts and changed his clothes, then headed inside. He didn't want to go into the newsroom at the moment, since he'd not had the time set his camera and take any pictures of his fight with Carnage and the Chameleon. Peter really didn't need Jonah screaming at him at the moment. But he did need to make a phone call and his tired brain figured the *Bugle* was the best place to do it.

He found an empty office one floor above the newsroom that still had a desk and a live phone, and dialed Reed Richards's number.

Reed answered almost before the phone stopped its first ring. He'd told Spidey once that he carried that phone with him almost everywhere the Fantastic Four went. It had come in handy far too many times, he'd said. But at the moment Spidey had no idea in just what part of the world the phone was ringing. As it turned out it was in the Fantasti-Car headed back to New York.

"Reed Richards."

"Friendly neighborhood Spider-Man," Peter said in a like tone.

"Spidey!" Reed's voice sounded genuinely happy to

hear from him. "We're ten minutes from the city, but from what we saw, we're too late to help again. How are you doing?"

"Besides exhausted?" Spidey asked.

Reed laughed. "Yes, besides that."

"Good, actually. I found the vial."

There was a silence on the other end of the line. Peter could feel the huge relief flooding over the phone lines. It matched his own. Peter heard Reed turn from the phone line and say to someone behind him, "Spider-Man has Catrall's serum.

"That's wonderful," Reed said directly into the phone. "How? Where? Who had it?"

Spidey laughed. "I'll tell you the entire story when you get here." Spidey gave him the address of the old Osborn building and the directions on how to get into the hidden room in the basement.

"Ten minutes," Reed said and hung up.

Peter hung up the phone and let out a deep breath. Slowly the weight of the world was lifting from his shoulders.

He picked up the phone. He had to see how Mary Jane was doing and tell her he'd be home for dinner tonight.

Soon, he'd be able to sleep. Very soon.

After making sure Mary Jane was all right and telling her she'd get the entire story later, he managed to drag himself out of the chair and back to the roof. There he changed clothes again and beat the Fantastic Four to the old Osborn building by two minutes.

\* \* \*

Fifteen minutes later, Spidey had finished telling them the entire story, showing them the hidden Osborn office, the Goblin equipment and the still-dusty practice room. Then he and Reed left the other three members of the Fantastic Four to gather up Goblin equipment in the big room while they went into the dust-covered outer office.

"So where's the serum?" Reed asked.

"It was sitting right there on that desk," Spidey said, "when I found it." Spidey did a quick jump to a place near the ceiling and pulled out four books. From behind them, he carefully removed the vial and dropped back to the floor. He held it out for Reed.

Just as carefully, Reed took it from him, holding it up to the dim light.

"I think the Chameleon only used a few drops in the pumpkin bomb on the bridge."

Reed nodded, his face troubled by the mention of all the death. "We'll go over all the equipment we find in there to be sure. This is quite a powerful liquid," he said with acknowledged understatement.

Reed slipped a backpack he'd been carrying off his shoulder and placed it on the desk. Inside was what looked to be a standard briefcase. Reed pulled it out and opened it. Inside Spidey could see a padded interior with a place in the very center for the vial.

Reed placed the vial in the center and then pointed to the case. "A week ago I built this for when we found the serum."

"Positive thinking," Spidey said.

Reed laughed. "Wishful, more like it." Reed closed the case over the vial and locked it. Then he tapped the side. "It's adamantium. Hardest material known. Not even the Hulk could open this."

He stood the case up on end and Spidey could see a small computer screen under the handle. Reed pressed his finger against the computer screen and it beeped softly. A small red light came on and Reed picked up the case.

The light went to green.

"If this case is out of my grasp for longer than one minute," Reed said, "without my clearing the computer, the locks will fuse and no one will ever get the serum out of this case. I figured it was better that way."

Spidey laughed and applauded, feeling lighter and lighter as each moment went by. "I like your thinking."

The images of the river of blood flowing through the streets flashed in Spidey's head and then went away. Those pictures no longer haunted him, drove him as they had just this morning. There was no fear with them anymore.

Those images were now only a memory.

A very unpleasant memory of something he had stopped from happening.

Then the clear image of Gwen falling from that bridge filled his mind. He could still feel, even after all the years, her broken body in his arms. He pushed the thoughts of her away. He hadn't been able to save her. He was slowly learning to live with that fact.

But he'd saved Mary Jane. And today, that was what was important.

Spider-Man patted Reed Richards on the shoulder. "Can you handle this place?"

Reed smiled. "With pleasure. I think you've done more than enough today."

Spidey laughed. "Remember that nap I mentioned on your roof about two weeks ago?"

Reed nodded.

"I think I'll go take it now."

Spidey turned and headed for the door as behind him Reed Richards laughed a very relieved laugh.

\* \* \*

Two nights later, Peter, Mary Jane, Liz Osborn, and Flash Thompson surrounded a private table in the back of Antonio's Pizza. The remains of two large pepperoni pizzas filled the round table along with drinks and a huge old drip candle. Peter sat with his back against the wall. He couldn't remember a time over the last two years that he had laughed as much as he had tonight. Mary Jane had been right. He'd needed a night like this very much.

Antonio's had a thick smell of garlic and smoke that seemed to fill every nook and cranny of the dark, candle-lit restaurant. After eating at Antonio's, a person always smelled that thick Italian smell on their clothes for hours. It was one of Peter's favorite places, but lately they just hadn't had enough money to come here very often.

Today he'd gotten paid for the re-use of some old photos of Carnage and the Green Goblin the *Bugle* had used in the story about the fight. The money had been enough to buy them a nice dinner. Inviting Flash and Liz along had been Mary Jane's idea and when she suggested it, he actually felt good.

For two days after leaving the Fantastic Four in the old Osborn basement, Peter had slept and helped Mary Jane clean up their apartment. Reed had gotten the serum safely into a secure unit in his lab at Four Freedom's Plaza, and

Carnage was locked up solidly in the Vault again. There was no sign of the Chameleon and Peter doubted there would be for some time.

Mostly for the last two days he had thought of nothing but sleep and Mary Jane had encouraged him. Now, after a good meal, sitting in a safe, warm restaurant that he felt very comfortable in, he wanted even more sleep.

He leaned back in his chair, his back against the wall. With his eyes half closed, he took a few deep, relaxing breaths and looked fondly at his two friends and his beautiful wife, Mary Jane. They were chatting about the soap opera audition Mary Jane had coming up for next week. They weren't paying him the slightest attention.

For the moment he liked it that way.

He sighed and closed his eyes, letting the sounds of the restaurant wash over him like a lullaby. The dishes clicking in the kitchen. The buzz of distant conversations. The laughter of Mary Jane and his friends.

It wrapped around him like a warm quilt, telling him that for the moment all was safe.

Life was good. He was full and the bills were paid. He hadn't felt so relaxed in recent memory.

He yawned.

Just a little nap wouldn't hurt. Not a long one.

Just a few seconds. . . .

**Dean Wesley Smith** has sold around one hundred professional short stories and thirteen novels, but he claims that, since he was a comic fan for years, his favorite of those were his two *Spider-Man* novels, the other one being *Carnage in New York* (co-authored with David Michelinie). He has also published novels under his own name and under the name Sandy Schofield in the *Star Trek* and *Aliens* milieus, as well as in his very own universe. Dean was the editor of *Pulphouse: A Fiction Magazine* and currently edits the fiction section of *VB Tech Journal* in his spare time. He won the World Fantasy Award and has been nominated for the Hugo Award in Science Fiction four times.

\* \* \*

Rocketed to Earth as an infant, **James W. Fry** escaped the destruction of his homeplanet and grew to adulthood in Brooklyn, New York. In 1984, seduced by the irresistible combination of insane deadlines and crippling poverty, he embarked on a career as a freelance illustrator. James's credits include *The New ShadowHawk* for Image, *Star Trek* and *The Blasters* for DC Comics, *Moon Knight* and *Midnight Sons Unlimited* for Marvel, and Topps Comics's *SilverStar*. He has provided illustrations for several *Star Trek: The Next Generation* young adult novels, the *Spider-Man* novel *Carnage in New York*, and *The Ultimate Spider-Man* as well as the forthcoming Incredible Hulk novel *Abominations* and *The Ultimate X-Men*. Himself a leading cause of stress-related illness in comic book editors, James's greatest unfulfilled ambition is to get one full night of guilt-free sleep.

# SPIDER-MAN®